Ripley's

DINOSAURS

Believe It or Not!®

a Jim Pattison Company

Written by Rupert Matthews
Consultant Steve Parker

Publisher Anne Marshall

Editorial Director Rebecca Miles
Project Editor Lisa Regan
Editor Rosie Alexander
Assistant Editor Charlotte Howell
Picture Researchers James Proud, Charlotte Howell
Proofreader Judy Barratt
Indexer Hilary Bird

Art Director Sam South
Senior Designer Michelle Cannatella
Design Rocket Design (East Anglia) Ltd
Reprographics Juice Creative Ltd

www.ripleybooks.com

This edition 2013

Ripley's Dinosaurs and *Ripley's Wild Animals* also available as individual volumes

ISBN 978-1-60991-052-5

10 9 8 7 6 5 4 3 2 1

Library of Congress Cataloging-in-Publication Data is available.

Manufactured in China
in April 2013 by Leo Paper
1st printing

CONTENTS

DINOSAUR DAYS

PREHISTORIC PLANET

Could you have survived living with the dinosaurs? Would you have managed to escape the terrifying teeth of the *Tyrannosaurus*, or avoid the slashing claws of a *Velociraptor*? Even if you did, would you have been happy eating moss or ferns in this strange and bizarre place? Or could you have captured a baby dinosaur—and then roasted it for your supper? In this book you will learn all you need to know about the world of the dinosaurs.

Millions of years ago the world was a very different place. Dinosaurs stalked the Earth, other reptiles flew in the skies and swam in the seas, and the largest mammal around was the size of a badger.

Do the twist

This book is packed with cool pictures and awesome facts. It will teach you amazing things about dinosaurs, but like all Twists books, it shines a spotlight on things that are unbelievable but true. Turn the pages and find out more...

Tyrannosaurus

THE GREAT DEATH

Sixty-five million years ago, all the dinosaurs died out, along with many marine reptiles, flying reptiles, and other types of animal. However, a few creatures survived, including lizards, birds, insects, and our own ancestors—the early mammals. Which is just as well for us!

TWISTS

DINOSAUR BASICS

A MATTER OF FACTS

Striding across the ground, some of the largest, most incredible animals ever to walk the Earth made the ground shake with every thundering footstep. For over 160 million years, the dinosaurs were one of the most successful groups of animals our planet had ever seen... then they vanished.

The dinosaurs were a huge group of reptiles that lived all over the world. There were more than 700 different types of dinosaur. Some were enormous, but others were tiny. Many were slow and clumsy, a lot were fast and agile. Dinosaurs included several types of animal that looked utterly bizarre, and some that might not look unusual if they were alive today.

TOTAL TYRANNOSAURUS

- *Tyrannosaurus had very short arms with powerful two-clawed fingers. These were probably used to seize prey, but were too short to reach its mouth.*
- *The closest living relative to Tyrannosaurus is the plain old chicken!*
- *Tyrannosaurus could eat up to 500 pounds of meat in one sitting–that's equivalent to 2,000 burgers!*

PALEOICHNOLOGIST
A scientist who studies fossils of things left behind by animals, such as footprints and nests.

Found a new word? Big word alerts will explain it for you.

A pterosaur becomes lunch!

These books are all about "Believe It or Not!"—amazing facts, feats, and things that will make you go "Wow!"

PRIZE FIGHTERS

Power Struggles

Take a ringside seat at this fight of the era. Charging toward each other at top speed, a pair of *Triceratops* clash with a resounding "thwack." ...orns lock together, the ...und vibrates, as each ...s its strong shoulder ...cles to try to wrestle ...other backward into ...t. Battles between ...inosaurs would have ...en terrifying.

...only meat-eating ...at needed to fight. ...nt-eaters had to ... dinosaurs of the ...ies over territory, ...tus. Some used ...frills or feathers ...ivals, others had ...s to use in their ...every contest ...erious injury, but ...urs would have ...ese fights.

Yee-HAA!

Whip crack away

Seismosaurus and other sauropods had enormously long, whip-like tails that were controlled by powerful muscles. They could have used these tails to lash each other into defeat. Sauropods may also have used their necks to swing their heads and butt each other, in a similar way to giraffes today.

Ripley's Believe It or Not!

WHAT'S THE POINT?

Stegosaur tails all had a tip armed with long, sharp spikes called a "thagomizer." This unusual name was originally part of a joke in a 1982 cartoon by Gary Larson in which an unfortunate caveman called Thag has been killed by such a weapon. It is now used as an official term by paleontologists worldwide!

twist it!

COME HERE AND SAY THAT!

One family of dinosaurs had enormously thick bony domes on top of their skulls that were up to an incredible 8 inches thick. The family was given the name of pachycephalosaurs, which means "thick-headed-reptiles."

Daspletosaurus was a slightly smaller relative of Tyrannosaurus that had a gaping mouth filled with huge sharp-tipped teeth. In battles, these dinosaurs would try to bite each other's faces, often inflicting deep gashes, which have been found on some fossils.

Torosaurus had the largest (full) dinosaur skull, which was more than 8 feet long.

Triceratops means "three-horned face."

One of the most recognizable of all the dinosaurs, *Triceratops* was a plant-eating whopper that stood up to 10 feet tall and 30 feet in length. Its enormous skull could be one third the length of its body and its famous horns were probably used in mating rituals as well as for defense.

Triceratops had no front teeth, so its mouth looked like a turtle's beak.

Don't forget to look out for the "twist it!" column on some pages. Twist the book to find out more fascinating facts about dinosaurs.

Learn fab fast facts to go with the cool pictures.

Go to page 44 for more facts about the crazy creatures in this book

HOW TO SPOT A DINOSAUR

Dinosaurs shared the following features, which helped to make them undisputed rulers of the Earth:

- A long tail for balance that made it easier for them to run quickly.
- Straight legs that tucked underneath their bodies, making moving more energy efficient.
- A prong on the astragalus (a bone in the ankle) that allowed for the attachment of strong tendons to aid agile movement.
- A bulge on the humerus (a bone in the upper leg) that allowed for powerful muscles to be attached to aid fast running.

DINO FACTS

- The word "dinosaur" means "terrible lizard."
- The tallest dinosaurs were over 50 feet in height—that's as high as a five-story building—and weighed as much as ten elephants.
- The smallest dinosaurs were about the size of a chicken.
- The fastest dinosaurs could run at about 45 mph—that's faster than a racehorse.

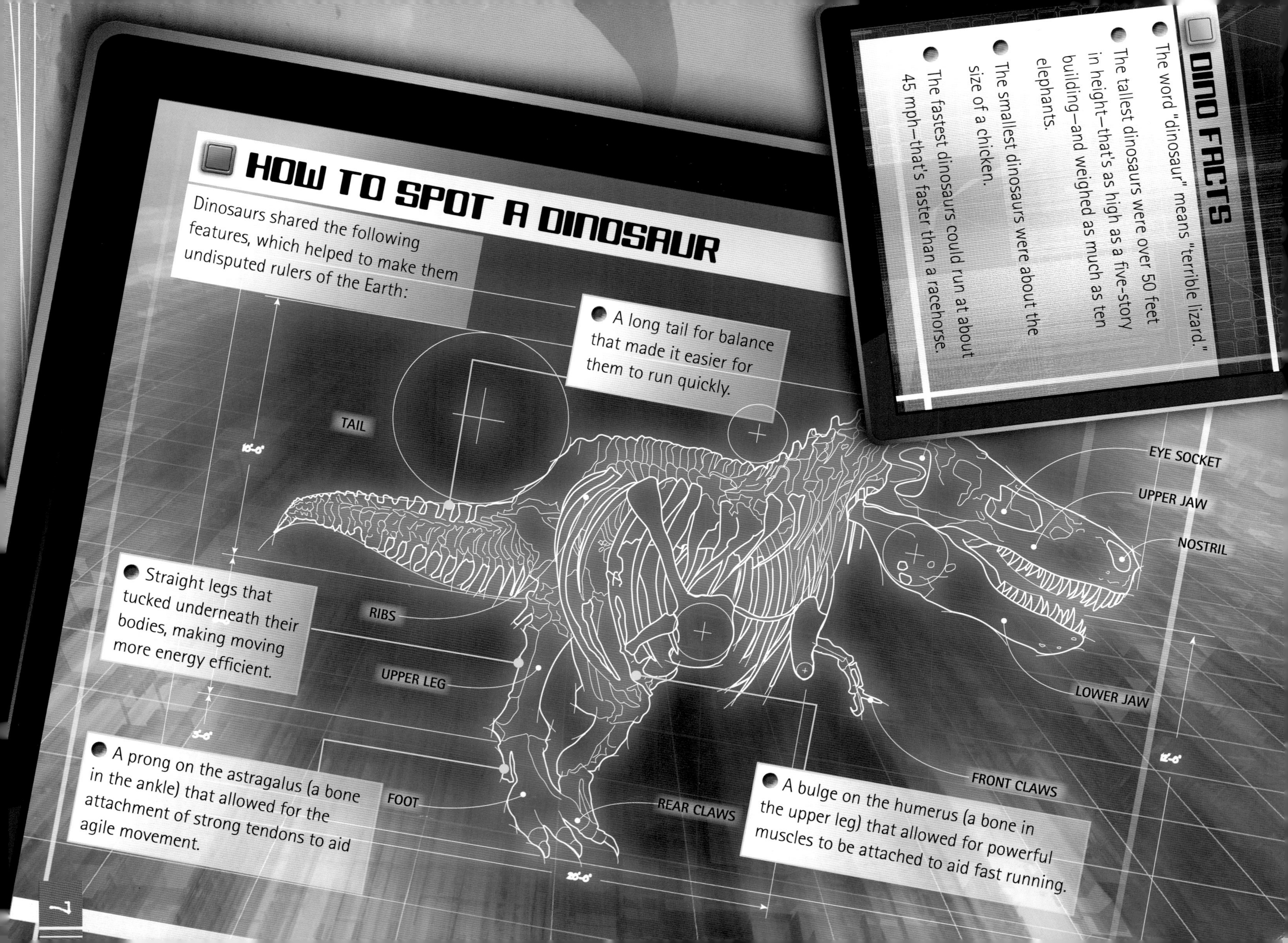

WATCH OUT!

STUDYING DINOSAURS

Scientists studying dinosaurs are constantly making new discoveries about these amazing creatures. Only recently they concluded that birds probably evolved from one dinosaur group, and that several groups of dinosaurs had feathers!

Looking at fossils can be a confusing business, especially as most dinosaur fossils found are not complete. But, as more and more fossils are unearthed, we learn more about dinosaurs and the world in which they lived. These incredible creatures were around for such a long time that some evolved and others became extinct millions of years apart.

MESOZOIC ERA
The time in which the dinosaurs lived, made up of the Triassic, Jurassic, and the Cretaceous Periods.

Pterosaur

Dinosaurs lived only on land, but they shared their world with flying reptiles called pterosaurs (see page 38) and several groups of water-dwelling reptiles (see page 40).

Diplodocus

This was one of the sauropod group of dinosaurs (see page 14). All sauropods were four-legged plant-eating giants and many had long whip-like tails.

The Time Lords

First signs of life 3.5 bya
First dinosaur 230 mya
First pterosaurs 220 mya
Diplodocus 155 mya
Stegosaurus 150 mya

Triassic period
Jurassic period

251 mya
bya = billion years ago
mya = million years ago
200 mya
145 mya
MESOZOIC ERA

HIP-HIP-ARRAY!

All dinosaurs belonged to one of two groups, based on the shape of their hip bones. One group had hips shaped like those of a modern reptile. These are called lizard-hipped dinosaurs, or saurischians. The other group had hips shaped like those of a modern bird, and are called bird-hipped dinosaurs, or ornithischians.

The bird-hipped dinosaurs were all plant-eaters. The lizard-hipped dinosaurs were divided into two further groups—theropods, who were all meat-eaters, and the sauropods, who were all plant-eaters with long necks and long tails.

Surprisingly, many scientists believe that birds today are descended from the lizard-hipped theropods, not from bird-hipped dinosaurs as you might expect.

Stegosaurus

Stegosaurus is famous for having a very small brain. Despite not being the brightest of dinosaurs, it was around for many millions of years.

Triceratops

Arriving on the scene just 3 million years before the dinosaurs' mass extinction, Triceratops is recognized by the shape of the horns and large bony frill on its head.

What's the Evidence?

The dinosaurs lived many millions of years ago. Not a single one is alive today, so there is no chance to study them in the wild or look at them in a zoo.

We know about dinosaurs only because scientists have found their remains buried in rocks. These remains are known as fossils and are usually the imprint of bones, teeth, and other hard parts of a dinosaur body. Muscles, organs, and other soft parts do not often get preserved as fossils. Scientists use the fossils to try to work out what the dinosaur looked like when it was alive. They study details on the dinosaur's bones to decide where its muscles, eyes, stomach, and other missing parts would have been.

When scientists reconstruct dinosaurs, they often have very little evidence to work with, but meat-eating Afrovenator, here, was found as a single almost complete skeleton. The dinosaur was 30 feet long from its nose to the tip of its tail.

Ripley's Believe It or Not!®

Bone home

Bone Cabin near Medicine Bay, Wyoming, is built completely from dinosaur bones. Thomas Boylan began collecting discarded bone fragments from a nearby dinosaur dig in 1916. By 1933, he had gathered 5,796 bones, which he then decided to use to construct a lodge measuring 29 feet long and 19 feet wide—that's the length of a Stegosaurus.

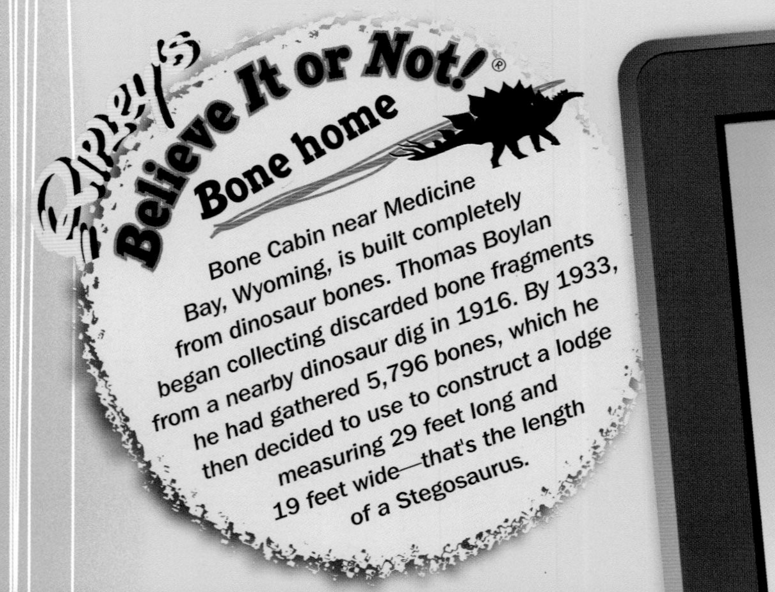

Saving Its Skin

Dinosaur skin was often scaly, as indicated by this fossil from the hindquarters of a *Triceratops* that died 65 million years ago in Hell Creek, Montana. Fossils rarely record accurate color, so scientists in the past guessed that dinosaur skin was dark green or brown, like crocodile or alligator skin. More recently, they have changed their minds and now think dinosaurs may have come in a rainbow of colors—some green, some red, and some even sporting spots or stripes!

Feathered friends

In 1997, Chinese scientists in Liaoning Province found the fossilized remains of a small hunting dinosaur named Caudipteryx. They were astonished to see that the dinosaur had been covered in feathers. This led many scientists to believe that birds evolved from dinosaurs.

What's in a name?

If scientists discover an entirely new type of dinosaur, they are allowed to give it a name. Most scientists use names from ancient Greek or Latin that describe a feature of the fossil, such as Triceratops, which means "three-horned face." Other scientists use the name of the place the fossil was found, the name of the person who found it, or even what the weather was like at the time!

Dig that

In 1909, scientist Earl Douglass discovered some dinosaur fossils near Jensen in Utah, USA. He began digging, and scientists haven't stopped since—they are still finding fossils there today. More than 10,000 dinosaur fossils have been discovered at this one site, which is now preserved as the Dinosaur National Monument.

HOW TO MAKE A FOSSIL

Take one newly dead dinosaur.

Leave for 1,000 years until its skeleton has been covered by deposits of mud or sand.

Allow layers of rocks, minerals, and even oceans to build up on top of the dinosaur, preserving its skeleton deep beneath the Earth's surface.

After 80 million more years the landscape changes and the rocks containing the dinosaur's fossilized remains are exposed once more.

SUCH A SOFTY

In 1981, an amateur paleontologist discovered this 113-million-year-old fossilized *Scipionyx* dinosaur in Italy. What makes it unique is that 85 percent of its body is intact, including its windpipe, muscles, intestines, and other internal organs.

BIG WORD ALERT

PALEONTOLOGIST
A scientist who studies fossils, animals and plants.

HOME SWEET HOME

DINOSAUR WORLD VIEW

CONTINENT
Any of the world's main continuous areas of land, such as Africa or Asia.

The world the dinosaurs inhabited was very different from our own. Strange plants grew on the ground and bizarre creatures swam in the seas or flew in the skies. Even the continents were in different places.

During the Triassic period, dinosaurs inland coped with throat-drying desert zones, while, during the Jurassic period, they enjoyed a warm, wet climate. The Cretaceous period had both warm and cool times, and huge, shallow seas spread over the planet. Their warm waters evaporated and fell as heavy rain on land. Vast forests started to grow. Some plants and insects we see today existed back then and provided dinosaurs with a variety of foods, such as leafy ferns, pine trees, mushrooms, magnolias, dragonflies, and tasty termites.

Pangaea

When the age of dinosaurs began, all the continents on Earth were joined together into a vast landmass that scientists call Pangaea, which means "all of earth." About 170 million years ago, Pangaea split in two, forming Laurasia and Gondwanaland. About 130 million years ago, Gondwanaland began to split up to form South America, India, Africa, Australia, and Antarctica. Laurasia divided about 50 million years ago into North America and Europe-Asia.

WHAT A STINK!

In Kawah Ijen, Indonesia, miners cover their mouths to protect against choking on sulfurous gas, as they pull stinking sulfur from a volcanic crater. The air dinosaurs breathed often must have been just as bad. Volcanic eruptions during the Mesozoic era pumped out huge quantities of sulfur and other evil-smelling gases. In wet areas, swamps containing rotting vegetation would have stunk. And don't even think about the terrible-smelling breath of the carnivorous dinosaurs, with rotten meat festering in their teeth.

Some of today's flora and fauna would have been known to the dinosaurs.

CALLING PLANET EARTH

The very first flowering plants appeared about 125 million years ago in eastern Asia, during the early Cretaceous period. Some 25 million years later, flowering plants suddenly spread right across the world and took over from earlier types of plants.

The climate of the world was at its hottest about 110 million years ago, when it was around 10°F warmer than it is today.

In the later Cretaceous Period vast volcanic eruptions spurted molten rock across India. An area of land about 600,000 square miles was covered in lava about 1¼ miles thick.

Where did you come from?

When fossils of the same animal are found on different continents it suggests that those continents were once joined together. This is because large land animals couldn't get across oceans and only traveled around by walking.

Fossils of the crocodile-like reptile Uberabasuchus—seen here having a dinosaur for dinner—have been found in South America, Africa, and Madagascar, suggesting how these landmasses were joined together about 100 million years ago.

HOW BIG?

Super Sauropods

Imagine if the sauropods—the biggest of all the dinosaurs—roamed our streets today. These gentle giants would be able to peer into windows five floors up and crush cars as if they were toys. They were the largest animals that have ever walked the Earth.

Sauropods swallowed stones and pebbles that remained in their stomachs. As the stomach muscles churned the food about, the stones pummeled the leaves and twigs to a mushy liquid that could be more easily digested in their huge intestines.

Argentinosaurus
About 100 feet long (head to tail)
Weighed a colossal 88 tons

Mamenchisaurus
About 43 feet long
Had a neck that was half its total body length

The sauropods were a group of plant-eating dinosaurs that had long necks and long tails. They had small mouths, so they had to eat almost continuously to consume enough food. They couldn't chew, so they had huge stomachs and intestines—filling most of their body—to process the leaves and twigs on which they fed. Sauropods first appeared about 200 million years ago and by 150 million years ago were the most important types of plant-eating dinosaurs.

Brachiosaurus
About 80 feet long
Could raise its neck 2–3 times higher than a giraffe

In the case of some sauropods, their head could be 26 feet above their heart. So they needed a large, powerful heart, weighing about 880 pounds—that's the weight of four average adult men—to pump blood up to the head.

Agustinia
About 50 feet long
Had bony spikes down its back, unlike most other sauropods

SMALL AND SAVAGE

MINI DINOSAURS

Some of the earliest dinosaurs were no larger than chickens! *Eoraptor* from the Triassic Period was about 3 feet long, and half of that was its tail. Some dinosaurs did evolve to be bigger and stronger, but others remained small. *Compsognathus*, from the Jurassic Period, was even smaller than *Eoraptor*.

Often running together in savage packs, the smaller hunters of the dinosaur world were deadly and terrifying. Armed with razor-sharp claws and teeth, they could run faster than anything else on Earth and bring down prey much larger than themselves with startling speed.

Velociraptor was one of the most intelligent dinosaurs. Its brain was relatively large in comparison to its body size.

Velociraptor was a smart turkey-sized predator. Although many images of this deadly hunter show it as a scaly reptile, we now know that it was actually covered in feathers and bird-like in appearance.

Velociraptor could run at speeds of up to 40 mph for short bursts.

Deadly battle

Velociraptor was not afraid to attack larger animals. In 1971, fossils were found in Mongolia that showed a *Velociraptor* and a *Protoceratops* buried together. They had been fighting and the *Protoceratops'* beak had bitten deep into the *Velociraptor*, which had been attacking the *Protoceratops* with its claws. They may have died in a sudden sandstorm or when a sand dune collapsed.

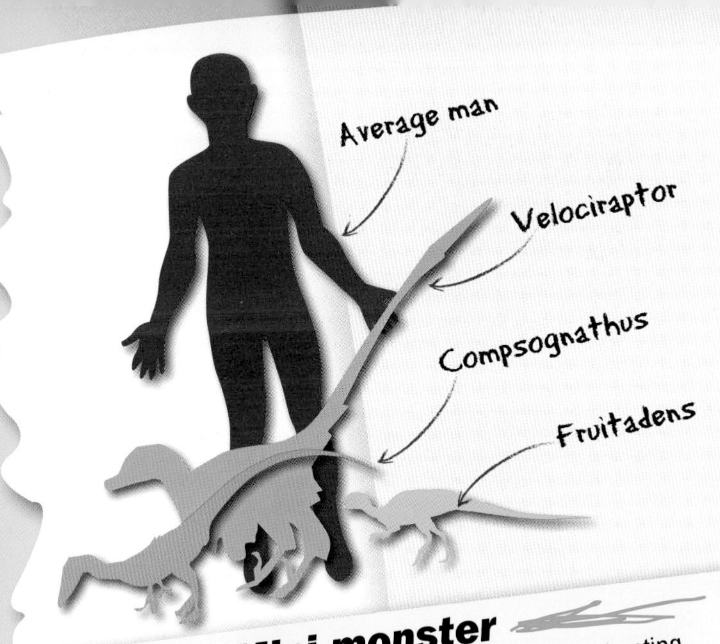

Mini monster

Microraptor got its name because it is one of the smallest hunting dinosaurs known—only 15 inches long. It had flight feathers along both its arms and on its legs, so it probably climbed trees and glided from one to another. It may have pounced on prey by gliding onto it.

Dozy dino

The dinosaur with the shortest name is 2-foot-long *Mei*. This little hunting dinosaur lived about 130 million years ago in eastern Asia. Its name means "sleepy" because the first fossil found of this dinosaur is in the pose of a sleeping bird with its head tucked under its arm.

Insect picker

Six-foot-long *Patagonykus* had only one claw on each arm. Powerful muscles were attached to its arms and scientists think that *Patagonykus* may have used its claw to rip open termite mounds so that it could feed on the insects inside.

Sniff sniff

Byronosaurus had nasal bones that show it was very good at smelling things. Perhaps this five-foot-long dinosaur hunted at night and used its sense of smell to find food.

HIGH FLYER

One of the most successful agile early hunters was *Coelophysis* (see page 25). Scientists have found hundreds of fossils of this dinosaur buried together. The skull of one *Coelophysis* was taken into space in 1998 by the space shuttle *Endeavour*.

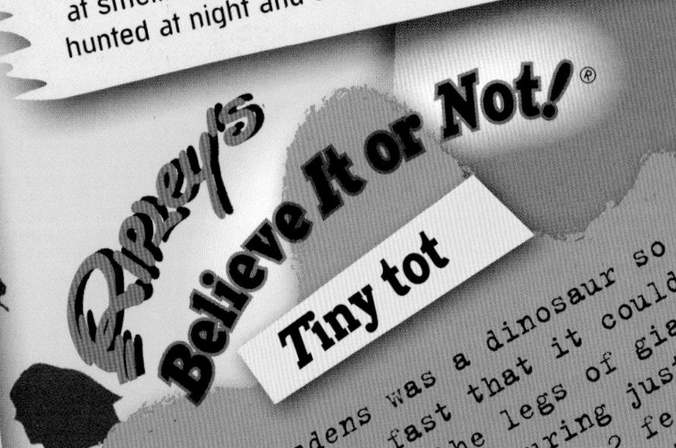

Ripley's Believe It or Not!®

Tiny tot

Fruitadens was a dinosaur so small and fast that it could dart between the legs of giant dinosaurs. Measuring just 12 inches tall and 2 feet from head to tail, it weighed the same as a guinea pig, and ate small animals, bugs, and plants for its dinner.

KNIGHTS IN ARMOR

Powerful Protection

Encased in almost as much armor as a modern battle tank, and bristling with spikes, horns, and clubs, armored dinosaurs were awesome animals. Even the most ferocious hunter would think twice about launching an attack on them.

The bony armor that covered so many different types of dinosaurs—mainly the ankylosaur and stegosaur groups—was so protective that often the only way a predator could cause injury was by flipping the dinosaur over and exposing the soft belly. Judging by the size and shape of these beasts, that would not have been easy!

Ankylosaurus had a massive double-headed club on its tail. It may have used this to bash away at the armored backs of rivals in disputes over territory or status. This 20-foot-long chunky reptile was a herbivore and had to eat a huge amount of plant material to sustain itself, so its gut was very large. It probably had a fermentation chamber in its gut to aid in the digestion process. This offered another form of protection—enormous amounts of gas!

On a plate

All armored dinosaurs belong to one large group called the Thyreophora. Within the Thyreophora are the stegosaurs, ankylosaurs, scutellosaurs, and emausaurs. Many fossils of these dinosaurs are found upside down, as if a hunter had flipped them over to get to their less protected underbelly, and then used the shell as a plate from which to eat the juicy meat.

A LOT ON ITS PLATE

One of the earliest known armored dinosaurs, *Scutellosaurus* lived about 200 million years ago in the early Jurassic period. Only 4 feet long, it had more than 300 plates of bony armor—called scutes—set into its skin.

Blinking hard

Euoplocephalus was so heavily armored that even its eyelids were covered in bone. If provoked, all its armor may have filled with blood and turned pink.

twist it!

KEEP OUT!

Given the weight of all that armor, ankylosaurs and stegosaurs were slow-moving creatures that walked on four legs. However, with all that protection, there was little need to be able to run away from predators.

Ankylosaurs and stegosaurs all belonged to the larger Thyreophora group of dinosaurs, all of which only ate plants. Thyreophora means "those who carry large shields."

Yingshanosaurus was a stegosaur with a pair of huge spikes on its shoulders, each about 4 feet long. Unfortunately, the Chinese scientist who found the fossil has now lost it, so nobody can be certain what the dinosaur looked like.

Sharp practice

Chialingosaurus was a smaller relative of *Stegosaurus*. It had bony plates on its neck and upper back, and spikes on its lower back and tail. As it was modestly sized, weighing just 500 pounds and measuring 13 feet in length, it might have been able to rear up on its hind legs and present a wall of spikes.

PRIZE FIGHTERS

POWER STRUGGLES

Take a ringside seat at this fight of the era. Charging toward each other at top speed, a pair of *Triceratops* clash with a resounding "thwack." Horns lock together, the ground vibrates, as each uses its strong shoulder muscles to try to wrestle the other backward into defeat. Battles between rival dinosaurs would have been terrifying.

It was not only meat-eating hunters that needed to fight. Many plant-eaters had to fight other dinosaurs of the same species over territory, food, or status. Some used displays of frills or feathers to scare off rivals, others had real weapons to use in their battles. Not every contest ended with serious injury, but some dinosaurs would have died in these fights.

COME HERE AND SAY THAT!

One family of dinosaurs had enormously thick bony domes on top of their skulls that were up to an incredible 8 inches thick. The family was given the name of pachycephalosaurs, which means "thick-headed-reptiles."

Daspletosaurus was a slightly smaller relative of *Tyrannosaurus* that had a gaping mouth filled with huge sharp-tipped teeth. In battles, these dinosaurs would try to bite each other's faces, often inflicting deep gashes, which have been found on some fossils.

Torosaurus had the largest frilled dinosaur skull, which was more than 8 feet long.

Whip crack away

Seismosaurus and other sauropods had enormously long, whip-like tails that were controlled by powerful muscles. They could have used these tails to lash each other into defeat. Sauropods may also have used their necks to swing their heads and butt each other, in a similar way to giraffes today.

Ripley's Believe It or Not!®

WHAT'S THE POINT?

Stegosaur tails all had a tip armed with long, sharp spikes called a "thagomizer." This unusual name was originally part of a joke in a 1982 cartoon by Gary Larson in which an unfortunate caveman called Thag has been killed by such a weapon. It is now used as an official term by paleontologists worldwide!

Triceratops means "three-horned face."

One of the most recognizable of all the dinosaurs, *Triceratops* was a plant-eating whopper that stood up to 10 feet tall and 30 feet in length. Its enormous skull could be one third the length of its body and its famous horns were probably used in mating rituals as well as for defense.

Triceratops had no front teeth, so its mouth looked like a turtle's beak.

PALEOICHNOLOGIST
A scientist who studies fossils of things left behind by animals, such as footprints and nests.

FINDING YOUR FEET

Ferocious Footwear

Equipped with vicious claws, curving talons, or ponderous pads, dinosaur feet came in a variety of shapes and sizes. The design of their feet and legs was essential to the dinosaurs' success and made them the rulers of the world.

Dinosaur legs were positioned directly under their bodies, so the weight of the animal rested on the bones. In other reptiles, the legs splayed sideways, so the animal used more energy to work its muscles to lift its body off the ground. This meant that dinosaurs could move more efficiently than other animals when looking for food or escaping from danger, and this was enough to give them control of the Earth.

Big foot!

The feet of the biggest dinosaurs needed to be absolutely huge to support their massive weight. This scaled-down drawing shows how they compared to creatures of today.

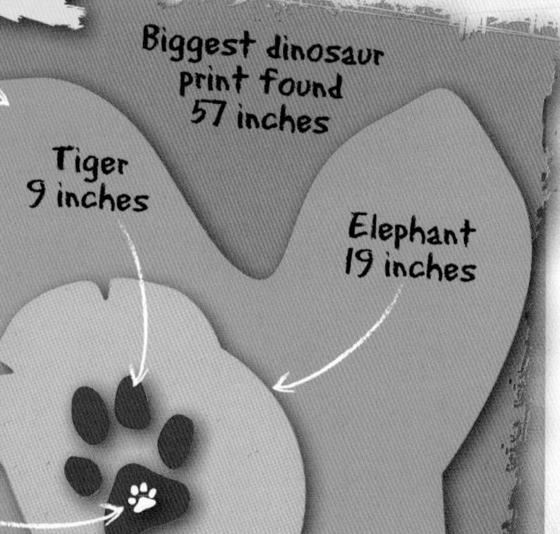

That's gotta hurt

The thumb of the plant-eater Iguanodon took the form of a stout, very sharp spike. It may have been used in fights between rival Iguanodon.

Gone fishing

The front foot of Baryonyx carried a huge, curved claw. This may have been used to help the dinosaur catch fish from rivers or lakes.

The sauropod group of giant dinosaurs was named because of the arrangement of the bones inside their feet. "Sauropod" means "lizard foot."

Take cover!

Imagine this huge claw bearing down on your flesh. It sat, ready to rip, on the hind leg of *Deinonychus*. Only when the fossils of this dinosaur were discovered in the 1960s did scientists wise up to the fact that some dinosaurs had been fast, agile, and lethal. Before this, they thought dinosaurs had all been slow, lumbering beasts.

Claws call

The hind legs of **Allosaurus** *and some other hunters carried three large claws, which were connected to powerful muscles. These may have been used to kick victims to death.*

No escape

The gigantic, grasping hands of **Deinocheirus** *were tipped with terrible 10-inch-long claws. On the end of 8-foot-long forelimbs, they were the ultimate far-reaching weapon.*

Utterly useless

The front legs of **Tyrannosaurus** *were so small that they could reach neither the ground nor the mouth. They could not even have been used to scratch itches.*

Some dinosaurs had feet or claws designed for very specific purposes. Others, such as the mighty *Tyrannosaurus*, had powerful hind legs but surprisingly useless front legs.

ARMED TO THE TEETH

Open Mouths

Sharper than a steak knife and bigger than a dagger, the teeth of the immense hunter dinosaurs were ferocious weapons. Other dinosaurs had broad, flat teeth that were able to crush bones to powder. Plant-eaters had teeth designed for slicing, chopping, and grinding.

We can use fossilized teeth to discover what sort of food a dinosaur ate. If the jaws are found intact, they can show how the teeth were used when the dinosaur was feeding. Dinosaur teeth can also show who ate who in the dinosaur world. Scientists have found marks that match the teeth of a *Tyrannosaurus* on the bones of a *Triceratops*. And the broken off tip of an *Allosaurus* tooth has been found stuck in a sauropod bone.

Your point is?

One of the largest dinosaur teeth ever discovered was 11 inches long. It was found in North America and had a sharp point as it came from a meat-eater. Because the tooth was found on its own, nobody can be certain what type of dinosaur it came from.

LARGEST DINOSAUR TOOTH EVER FOUND

TROODON TOOTH

HUMAN INCISOR

SMALL TYRANNOSAURUS TOOTH

LION TOOTH

SMALL MEGALOSAURUS TOOTH

LARGE MEGALOSAURUS TOOTH

ALL TEETH ACTUAL SIZE

Tusk force

Heterodontosaurus had two pairs of long, sharp tusks near the front of its mouth, and smaller, grinding teeth at the rear of the jaws. It is thought that it used the tusks to dig up roots that were then chewed by the rear teeth.

Toothless

The fast-running ornithomimid dinosaurs had no teeth at all! Instead they had a beak, like that of a modern bird. It is thought that they ate lizards, beetles, and small animals.

Duck!

Gryposaurus had a giant, duck-like bill packed with hundreds of teeth. The 30-foot-long plant-eater had 300 teeth inside its beak, with a further 500 in its jaw ready to grow as replacements.

SMILE PLEASE

The huge sauropod *Supersaurus* was one of the largest dinosaurs ever, but it had very small teeth. The adult animal was about 105 feet long, but each tiny tooth was only 1¼ inches long. That's like an adult human having teeth no thicker than a grain of rice.

Hadrosaurs had massive rows of grinding teeth in their jaws to chew the tough plants that they ate. On average, each hadrosaur had about 4,000 teeth in its jaws.

The largest dinosaur tooth found still in its owner's jaws belonged to a *Daspletosaurus*. The tooth was 8.6 inches long and 1.2 inches wide. Slightly curved and found at the front of the mouth, it was probably used to tear lumps of meat from a victim.

Tyrannosaurus had teeth up to 12 inches long. Each tooth was narrow and edged with serrations that would have torn through flesh like a meat knife.

twist it!

Jagged edge

Coelophysis was one of the earliest dinosaurs and lived in the late Triassic period. It was an excellent hunter that could run fast and dart from side to side. Its sharp, curved, jagged teeth were perfect for gripping and eating small animals.

ON THE MENU

DINOSAUR DINNERS

Gobbling up everything in sight, the giant dinosaurs stomped across the world consuming enormous amounts of food. They then deposited great big, stinking droppings behind them.

It is very difficult for scientists to estimate just how much different dinosaurs ate. The amount eaten would depend on the nutritional value of the food available, how efficient the dinosaur's body was at digesting the food, and how active they were. Fortunately, some dinosaur droppings have been fossilized and can be studied. They are known as coprolites.

Little taste

The alvarezsaurid family of dinosaurs may have eaten termites, ants, and other insects. They would have needed to eat several thousand every day.

CARNIVORE CUISINE

COCKTAIL OF THE HOUR

Swamp water at sundown

STARTER

Mixed mammal salad drizzled with blood

TODAY'S CATCH

Sea-trawled Elasmosaurus neck fillets, on a bed of volcanic ash

MAIN COURSE

Sauropod steak topped with an Oviraptor egg

DESSERT

Fried dragonflies with termite sauce

Spinosaurus was a large deadly meat-eater that grew up to 60 feet in length and hunted alone. It had a preference for enormous fish and delicious fleshy chunks that it tore from the flanks of big dinosaurs with its crocodile-like jaws.

How rude!

Some animals regurgitated and spat out indigestible parts of food that they ate. Hunters may have eaten small animals whole, then spat out the bones. When these items are found as fossils they are known as "regurgitaliths."

GOING VEGGIE

APERITIF
Freshly squeezed moss juice, served with pine pretzels

SOUP OF THE SEASON
Sun-roasted fern

MAIN COURSE
Fungal flambée, sulfur-smoked cycad cones, with a side order of tossed horsetails

DESSERT
Stripped twig roulade with magnolia flower garnish

Stones will be provided for swallowing and aiding digestion

What tickled the fancy of Stegosaurus were ferns, mosses, cycads, and baby evergreen trees. Good job, its neck was too short to reach any tall plants. These were nutritiously poor plants so Stegosaurus would have had to spend all day grazing in order to get enough nutrients to survive.

Puzzling flavor

Monkey puzzle trees evolved about the same time as the earliest plant-eating dinosaurs. They produce a fruit about the size of a football that is filled with tasty, nutritious seeds.

A pile of dinosaur dung 130 million years old was sold at a New York auction for $960 in April 2008. The fossilized dung, from the Jurassic period, was bought by Steve Tsengas of Fairport Harbor, Ohio.

Christmas lunch

The Picea spruce tree evolved about 100 million years ago and was probably a favorite food of the crested hadrosaur dinosaurs. It is still around today, but is better known as the Christmas tree.

Poo goes there?

Coprolites from many different dinosaur species have been found, but scientists find it very difficult to work out which dinosaur the poo originally came from, unless the coprolite was found inside a particular dinosaur's skeleton.

A street in the town of Felixstowe in England is called Coprolite Street!

RIP ROARERS

PRIZE PREDATORS

Talons outstretched to slash at prey, the hunter raced across the landscape with its eyes focused on its intended victim. Once the prey was reached, a rip with the claws brought it down, after which it was quickly killed. Then the great teeth began to tear into the flesh.

Allosaurus grew up to 40 feet long—that's the size of a school bus!

Some of the hunting dinosaurs combined large size and immense strength with the ability to run quickly and change direction with extreme agility. They had long hind legs, powered by strong leg and hip muscles, as well as large, curved claws on their small front legs.

This baby sauropod didn't stand much chance against these lethal predators.

PREY
An animal that is hunted and killed by another animal for food.

JURASSIC LUNCH

This mighty mean *Allosaurus* doesn't look like he wants to share his lunch with the group of *Ceratosaurus* that have joined him in the late Jurassic forests of North America. Although *Allosaurus* hunted large plant-eating dinosaurs, such as the sauropod here, scientists think it may also have preyed on other predators, including *Ceratosaurus*—so these guys had better watch out!

RUUUUUN!

More than 50 *Allosaurus* skeletons have been found—this is one of the highest numbers of fossil skeletons for any Jurassic dinosaur. About 70 percent of all big dinosaur hunters in North America 155 million years ago are believed to have been *Allosaurus*.

The hunter *Saurophaganax* is the state mascot of Oklahoma, where it was found. It was similar to *Allosaurus*, but even bigger.

Dinosaur footprints found at Glen Rose in Texas show a pack of four *Acrocanthosaurus* hunters stalking a herd of sauropods. There is even a track indicating that one of the hunters kicked at a prey with its hind leg.

A piece of fossilized skin from the hunter *Carnotaurus* shows that it had round, pebble-like scales interspersed with bony cones on its body.

TWIST IT!

With razor-sharp teeth and horns, Ceratosaurus was just as scary as its deadly rival.

Ceratosaurus had a horn on the end of its nose and two smaller ones above its eyes. It grew to be 18 feet long and had a flexible tail that it could lash about.

BEAUTY AND THE BEASTS

SHOW-OFFS

It is safer for any animal to frighten off a rival or an attacker, rather than to fight. Even a strong beast might get hurt in a battle. By looking as big and as tough as possible, a dinosaur could frighten off a predator or challenge a rival of the same species.

Some dinosaurs were real show-offs, sporting wonderful, colorful plates, gigantic head crests, and multicolored tails. But these flourishes weren't just for fun. Dazzling dinosaurs wanted to bully and intimidate other animals, to protect themselves, get food, or attract a mate.

Moody Beast

The large bone plates on the back of *Stegosaurus* were covered in skin carrying large numbers of blood vessels. It is thought that the *Stegosaurus* could have changed the colors of the large plates to show what kind of mood it was in.

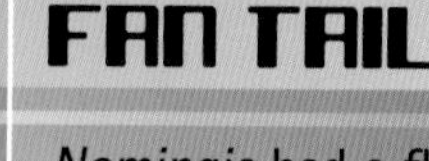

Nomingia had a flesh-covered bone protrusion on the end of its tail, just like that of a modern peacock. Scientists think that it had a large fan of brightly colored feathers that it could lift up and wave around in a threatening manner.

Twin Peak

Dilophosaurus was a 20-foot-long hunter that lived in North America about 190 million years ago. On top of its head the dinosaur had twin crests of paper-thin bone. These may have been brightly colored to act as signaling devices.

CROWNING GLORY

Styracosaurus, a large plant-eater that lived in the Cretaceous period, had a massive six-spiked frill projecting from the back of its skull, which might have been used in mating rituals and for scaring off rivals. These rivals could have included the mighty meat-eaters *Albertosaurus* and *Daspletosaurus*, who were around at the same time as *Styracosaurus*.

Fancy Flyers

Some scientists think that the wings of pterosaurs may have been brightly colored. Reptile skin can take on shades of red, blue, or green, so the wings may have been as showy as those of modern parrots.

Boat or Dinosaur?

Spinosaurus (see page 26) had a sail of skin about 5 feet tall along its back. The dinosaur could have turned sideways to face a rival, flashing its brightly colored sail to make itself look as big as possible.

FLAG WAVERS

Several types of hadrosaur, such as this *Parasaurolophus*, had bone crests that pointed back from their heads. Some think that flaps of brightly colored skin connected the crest to the neck. By waggling its head, the dinosaur could wave these flaps as if they were flags.

Big Head

Torosaurus had the largest skull of any land animal that ever lived. It was over 8 feet long, and most of the skin covering it was made up of a neck frill, which would have been brightly colored.

ON THE MOVE

Herds and Migration

Plodding along in vast herds, scampering in the undergrowth alone, or waiting in ambush for a victim, dinosaurs were active animals leading dangerous lives in hostile places.

All dinosaurs had to find food, escape enemies, seek shelter from weather, and find mates. Most did not live alone, but moved about their environment in different ways. Some lived in huge herds, such as the duck-billed dinosaur *Maiasaura*, whose fossils have been found in groups of about 10,000 animals. Others, like *Deinonychus* and *Velociraptor*, may have hunted in deadly packs, attacking even gigantic sauropods. Family groups were common, among *Centrosaurus* for example, while *Allosaurus* and other species may have lived solitary lives for much of the time.

WALL WALKING

Near Sucre, Bolivia, a vertical wall of limestone contains over 5,000 fossilized footprints left by some 250 dinosaurs.

The footprints were left in the mud around the edge of a lake about 70 million years ago.

Over time, the mud turned to rock, which was then twisted upright as the Andes mountains formed.

Now it looks as though the dinosaurs were walking up a wall.

Herd this?

About 68 million years ago, dozens of Centrosaurus were drowned trying to cross a flooded river. The bodies of the drowned herd were covered by mud and later became fossils. The archeologists who discovered the fossils, at Alberta's Dinosaur Provincial Park in Canada, found the remains of the dinosaurs spread over an area about the size of a football field.

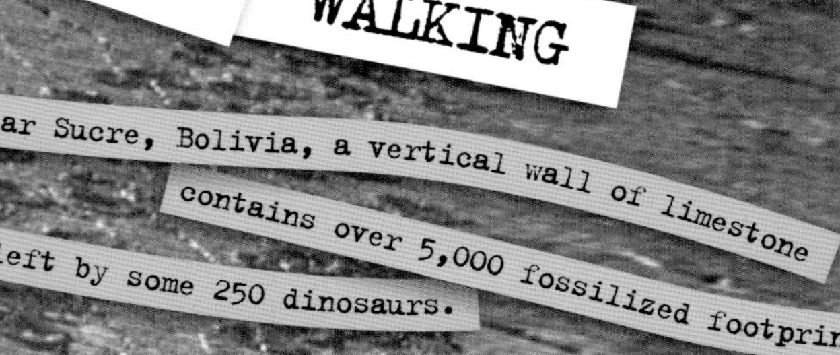

LIFE AS THEY KNEW IT

A large number of Triassic plant-eater *Plateosaurus* died crossing a desert that existed around what is now Trossingen, Germany. They were probably migrating from one food-rich area to another when they died.

Muttaburrasaurus is thought to have migrated 500 miles between its winter and summer grazing lands, in modern-day Australia.

In 2008, more than 1,000 dinosaur footprints were found on a ¾-acre site on the border of Utah and Arizona. Around 190 million years ago the area would have been a welcome watery oasis among hot, windswept sand dunes.

Twist it!

Baby Comes Too

A set of fossil footprints found at Culpeper, Virginia, showed a number of huge sauropods walking in a small group. The adults were on the outside of the group and the young on the inside. It seems the adults were protecting the young from some threat.

Ripley's Believe It or Not!®

Death by footprint

About 160 million years ago, a huge sauropod walked across a swamp in China leaving footprints 6 feet deep. Lots of smaller animals, including little *Limusaurus* dinosaurs, fell into the footprints, couldn't climb out, and died. Nine *Limusaurus* fossils were found in one of the footprints alone.

BIG WORD ALERT

MIGRATE To move regularly between two or more different places, either to find food or to find safe places to bring up young.

STOP THAT DINOSAUR!

BUILT FOR SPEED

Dinosaurs were not all lumbering beasts that just plodded around their world. The swiftest of the dinosaurs could give the cheetahs and antelopes of today a run for their money. With pounding feet and awesome power, running dinosaurs could disappear into the distance in seconds.

Speed is useful for any animal, whether it's trying to catch prey or escape from a hunter. Most swift animals live on open plains with few hiding places, so they need to move quickly. Fast dinosaurs probably lived in dry, open areas with no trees and little vegetation.

The fastest dinosaurs were the ornithomimosaurs, such as 12-foot-long *Dromiceiomimus*.

No way!

At this site near Cameron, Arizona, one man tries unsuccessfully to match the fossilized stride of a dinosaur predator that was as fast as an Olympic athlete.

LONG-LEGS

The ornithomimosaurs were large ostrich-like creatures, some of which ate meat.

Speed check

Cheetah 60 mph

Dromiceiomimus 50 mph

Tyrannosaurus 25 mph

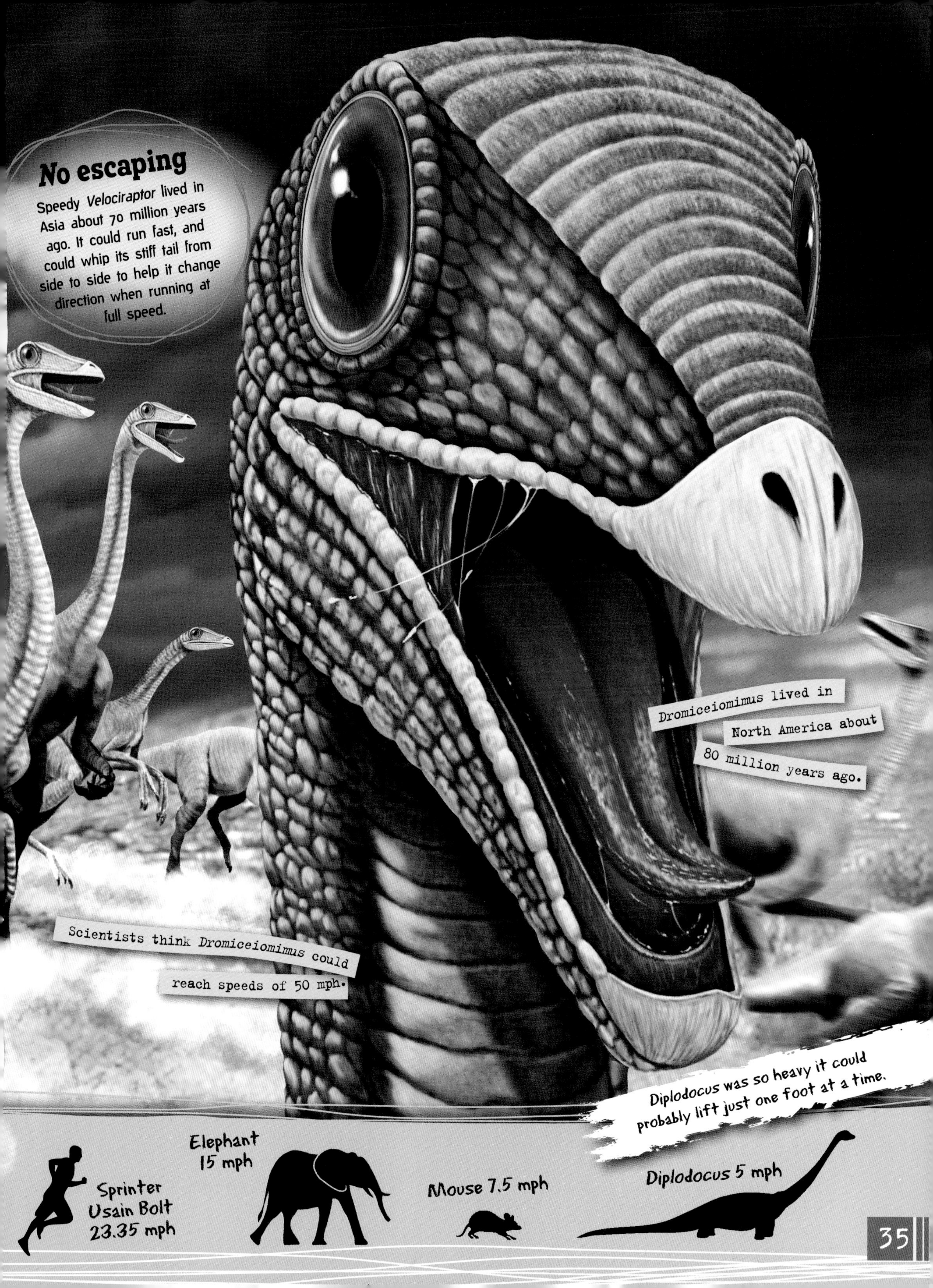
No escaping
Speedy *Velociraptor* lived in Asia about 70 million years ago. It could run fast, and could whip its stiff tail from side to side to help it change direction when running at full speed.
Dromiceiomimus lived in North America about 80 million years ago.
Scientists think *Dromiceiomimus* could reach speeds of 50 mph.
Diplodocus was so heavy it could probably lift just one foot at a time.
Sprinter Usain Bolt 23.35 mph
Elephant 15 mph
Mouse 7.5 mph
Diplodocus 5 mph

BIG MAMA

Newborns

All dinosaurs laid eggs, but working out their nesting behavior is very difficult. Scientists need to find fossils of a dinosaur's nests, eggs, and young to study, and, even then, it can be hard to piece together the mother's behavior.

Some dinosaurs built very carefully constructed nests in which to lay their eggs, and would have worked hard to find the ideal spot. Once the eggs were laid, some mothers would have guarded them against dangers, fed the babies when they hatched, and may even have looked after their young for months or years to come. Others walked away and let the hatchlings take their chances.

Giant egg nest

Seen here with an ordinary-sized chicken's egg, this is a nest of fossilized dinosaur eggs that was found in France. It isn't known which dinosaurs the eggs belonged to, but it looks like it must have been a lot bigger than a chicken!

Dinosaur auction

A nest of dinosaur eggs dating back 65 million years was sold at auction in Los Angeles in 2006 for $420,000. The nest, which was discovered in southern China in 1984, held 22 broken eggs, with some of the tiny unhatched dinosaurs clearly visible curled up inside. It was arranged in a circular pattern with the eggs placed along the edge. Scientists think it belonged to an oviraptor.

BIG WORD ALERT

INCUBATE
To keep eggs warm while the babies develop inside.

Baby dinosaurs grew very quickly and in some cases increased in size 16,000 times before reaching adulthood.

Triceratops laid its eggs in a spiral, *Maiasaura* in a circle. Sauropods left them in a row, as though the dinosaur laid them as she walked.

The smallest dinosaur eggs were about 1 inch across. They came from the small plant-eater *Mussaurus*.

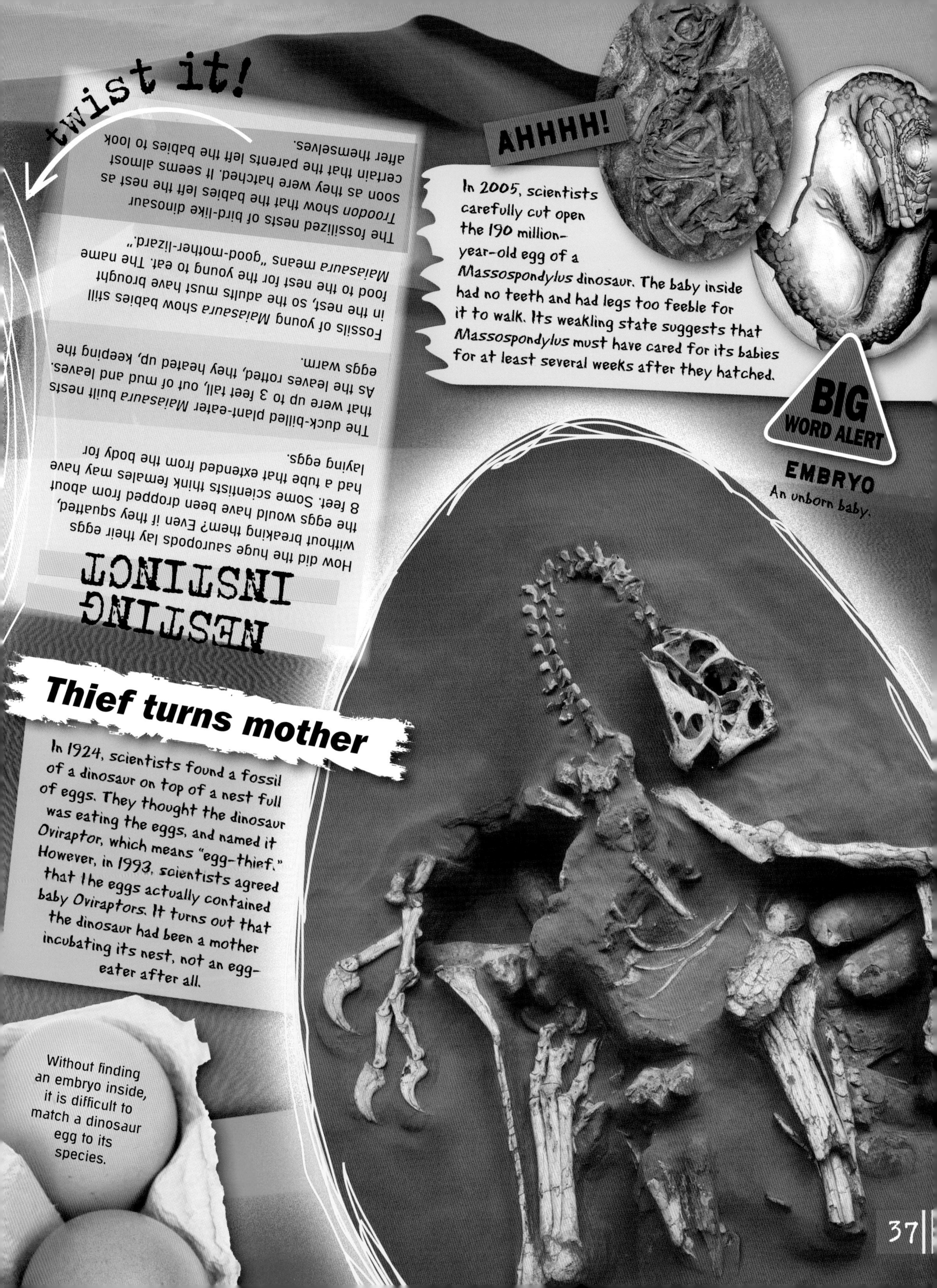

twist it!

NESTING INSTINCT

How did the huge sauropods lay their eggs without breaking them? Even if they squatted, the eggs would have been dropped from about 8 feet. Some scientists think females may have had a tube that extended from the body for laying eggs.

The duck-billed plant-eater *Maiasaura* built nests that were up to 3 feet tall, out of mud and leaves. As the leaves rotted, they heated up, keeping the eggs warm.

Fossils of young *Maiasaura* show babies still in the nest, so the adults must have brought food to the nest for the young to eat. The name *Maiasaura* means "good-mother-lizard."

The fossilized nests of bird-like dinosaur *Troodon* show that the babies left the nest as soon as they were hatched. It seems almost certain that the parents left the babies to look after themselves.

AHHHH!

In 2005, scientists carefully cut open the 190 million-year-old egg of a *Massospondylus* dinosaur. The baby inside had no teeth and had legs too feeble for it to walk. Its weakling state suggests that *Massospondylus* must have cared for its babies for at least several weeks after they hatched.

BIG WORD ALERT

EMBRYO
An unborn baby.

Thief turns mother

In 1924, scientists found a fossil of a dinosaur on top of a nest full of eggs. They thought the dinosaur was eating the eggs, and named it *Oviraptor*, which means "egg-thief." However, in 1993, scientists agreed that the eggs actually contained baby *Oviraptors*. It turns out that the dinosaur had been a mother incubating its nest, not an egg-eater after all.

Without finding an embryo inside, it is difficult to match a dinosaur egg to its species.

SKY PATROL

FLYING REPTILES AND BIRDS

The pterosaurs were a large group of flying reptiles that lived at the same time as the dinosaurs. They came in all shapes and sizes, ranging from gigantic gliders to small, agile flappers.

Soaring high above the ground, these flying reptiles twitched their great wings to swoop in a giant circle through the sky. Scanning the ground for the carcasses of a dead dinosaur, the pterosaurs sniffed the air for the tell-tale stink of rotting flesh.

About 150 million years ago, the first birds evolved and began to take to the air. They gradually replaced the pterosaurs as the most important flying creatures, until only a few pterosaurs were left alive by the time of the great extinction 65 million years ago.

Feathered friends

The fossil of a strange, feathered dinosaur from the middle to late Jurassic period—just before birds evolved—has been discovered in China. The pigeon-like creature, called Epidexipteryx, had four long ribbon-like tail feathers, which were probably used for display, but had no flight feathers. This fossil suggests that feathers were probably used for decoration millions of years before they were modified for flight.

The modern-day bat is the only mammal around today that is capable of sustained flight, and its wings share many of the characteristics of a pterosaur wing.

The pterosaur Pterodaustro had over a thousand bristle-like teeth in its jaws—about 62 per inch. It used these to filter tiny food particles from water.

These *Pteranodon* pterosaurs had huge, toothless bills, with which they caught their fish dinners, and wingspans of up to 30 feet.

Bats' wings are made from a fine membrane that connects their body to their arms and their long spread-out fingers. Pterosaur wings were made of a tough skin, but were attached to their bodies, arms, and fingers in a similar way. Birds, on the other hand, fly by using a row of feathers attached to each of their arms.

Ripley's Believe It or Not!®

Giant glider

One of the largest of the pterosaurs was Quetzalcoatlus, which lived in North America about 72 million years ago. It had a wingspan of 36 feet—that's the same as some small aircraft.

One of the early birds

Confuciusornis was a primitive bird that lived about 120 million years ago in eastern Asia. It was about the size of a modern crow and had long tail feathers that ended in wide flags. Its fossils provide evidence of a strong link between dinosaurs and birds.

The smallest known pterosaur was Nemicolopterus, which lived in forests in eastern Asia about 120 million years ago. It was about the size of a modern blackbird with a wingspan of just 9 inches.

WILD WATERS

Sea Monsters

Fossils of ichthyosaurs sometimes contain round, black pebbles near the rear of the body. It is thought that these are fossilized droppings and they are colored black by the ink found in the squid that the ichthyosaurs ate.

Help!

The dinosaurs also shared their world with several groups of water-dwelling reptiles, some of which were almost as big as them. These hungry sea giants powered their way through the waves snapping up fish, squid, ammonites, and other creatures in their tooth-fringed jaws. Some could even reach up into the air to grab flying pterosaurs on the wing.

Sea-going reptiles from the Mesozoic era included placodonts, ichthyosaurs, mosasaurs, plesiosaurs, and turtles. Some of these large water-dwelling reptiles died out before the dinosaurs did, others became extinct at the same time. There was one exception that lives on today: the turtles.

Living fossil?

A modern-day frill shark was found by a fisherman in Numazu, Japan, in 2007. Rarely seen out of its depth of 2,000 feet, this ancient-looking creature's body has many similarities to fossils of sharks that lived 350 million years ago.

Anyone for a swim?

A giant fossil sea monster found in the Arctic in 2008 had a bite that would have been able to crush a car. The marine reptile, which patrolled the oceans some 147 million years ago, measured 50 feet long and had a bite force of around 35,000 pounds.

Ripley's Believe It or Not!®

Big flipper

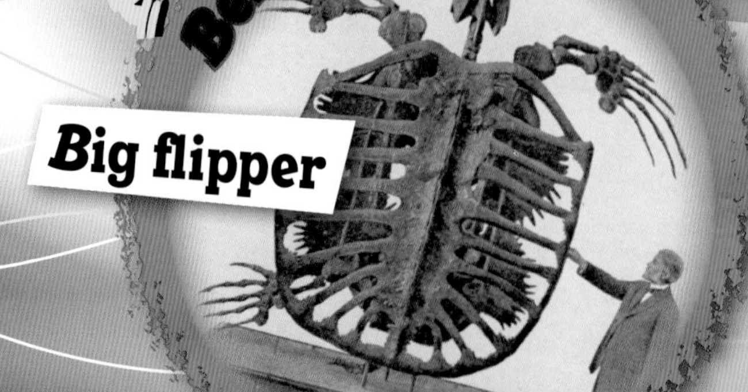

The fossils of the giant sea turtle *Archelon* date to around 75–65 million years ago, when a shallow sea covered most of North America. The largest specimen ever found is 13½ feet long and 16 feet wide from flipper to flipper.

Underwater flying

The plesiosaurs were a group of sea reptiles with stout bodies and four powerful flippers. They flapped their flippers in a similar way to how birds' wings work. *Pliosaurs* were massive plesiosaurs with short, powerful necks and sharp teeth. Some were more than 35 feet long and might have been able to rear up to catch passing pterosaurs or birds.

Supersize!

The biggest ichthyosaur was *Shonisaurus*, which grew more than 70 feet long. Scientists found the fossils of 37 of these monsters in one small area in Nevada. Perhaps a family group had become stuck on a prehistoric beach and died.

The 45-foot-long plesiosaur *Elasmosaurus* had more bones in its neck than any other animal that has ever lived—72 in all.

Amazingly, no complete fossil has been found that is as big as the blue whale that lives on Earth with us today.

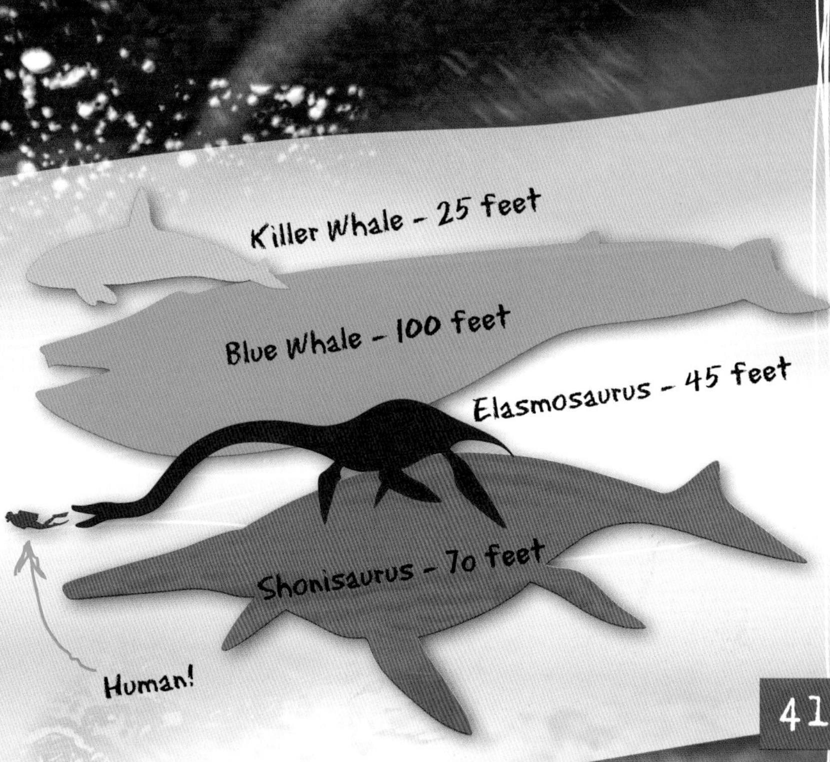

Killer Whale - 25 feet

Blue Whale - 100 feet

Elasmosaurus - 45 feet

Shonisaurus - 70 feet

Human!

DINO DT TIMES

WORLDWIDE EVENTS COMING TO YOU www.dinotimes 65 MILLION YEARS AGO

MASSIVE METEORITE HITS EARTH!

Scientists are agreed. Our planet has suffered a catastrophic meteorite hit in the Gulf of Mexico. Although reports are sketchy, as there is no sign of life in the immediate area, news is filtering through that the asteroid was about 6 miles wide and slammed into Earth at 43,000 miles per hour.

Reports suggest that, in just 30 seconds, the meteorite drilled a crater in Chicxulub, on the Yucatán Peninsula in Mexico, that was 24 miles deep and 125 miles wide. The meteorite collision has been compared to a blast from 100 megatons of high explosives.

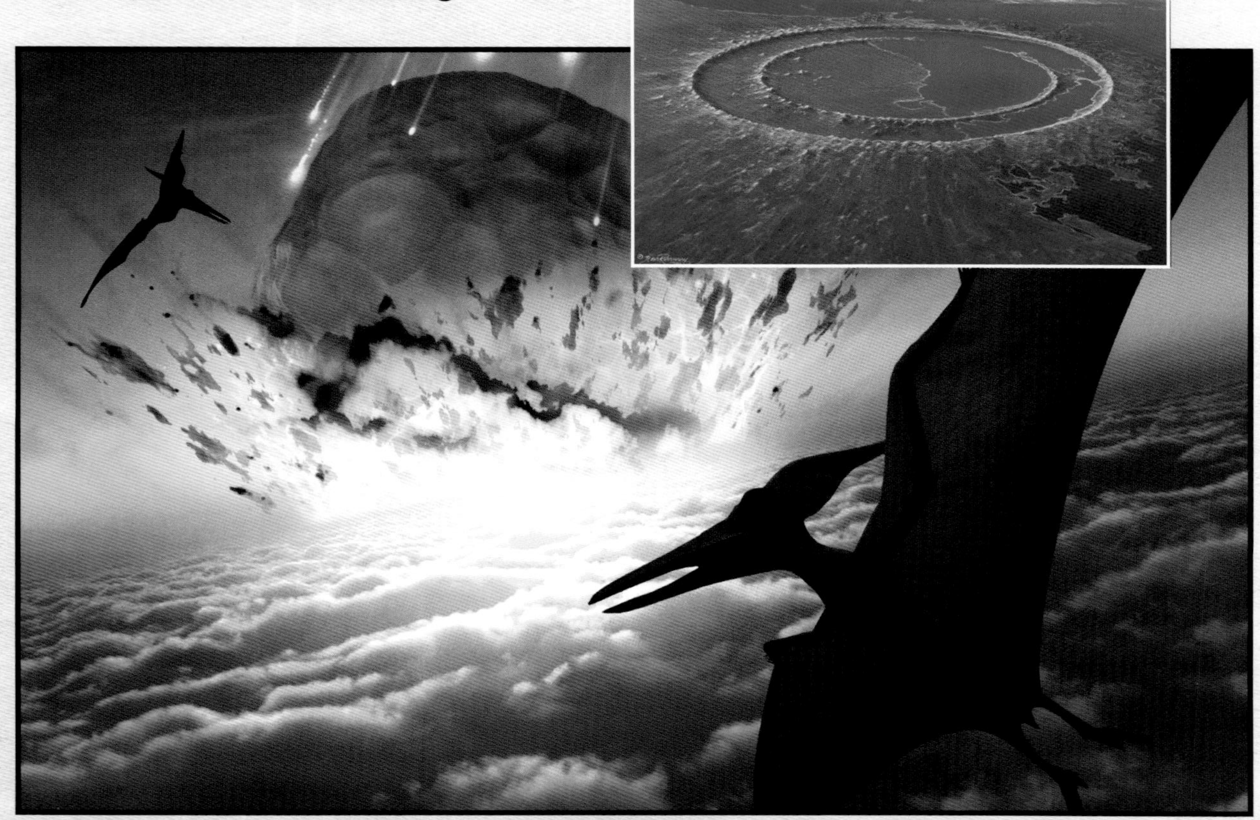

Where is the sun?

Dust thrown up from the meteorite impact is starting to block out sunlight. As a result, in many parts of the world, temperatures have dropped. Our dinosaur in the field has seen trees that are wilting and dying from lack of light. A *Triceratops* that depends on foliage for food moans, "We always have to eat a lot and now there's just not enough to go round."

Sightings of *Tyrannosaurus* and other meat-lovers gorging on weakened herbivores are becoming increasingly rare. "When the dark days first set in, forests began to die and dying herbivores were everywhere. Frankly, times were good," explains one. "But now their carcasses are starting to go off and we're panicking that fresh meat could be a thing of the past."

Hard to Breathe

Air quality is poor, as poisonous volcanic gases are becoming trapped under the dust clouds and ash continues to rain down. In some areas, gases have been acting like a lid on the world's atmosphere and have trapped in heat from volcanic activity. Rivers have dried and deserts are growing—all presenting more problems for plants and animals.

WEATHER WARNING!

Tsunamis, earthquakes, and hurricane winds imminent.

Today's Horoscope

Those born in the Mesozoic era will be confronting new challenges. Hold tight on booking next year's vacation.

JOKE OF THE DAY

What comes after extinction?
Y-stinction, of course!

Obituaries: Extinction has been announced of the following dinosaurs: Every single one.

DINO STATS

All the facts and figures on the main dinosaurs you'll find in this book.

KEY TO SYMBOLS

L = Length **H** = Height **W** = Weight

Herbivore (a plant-eating dinosaur)

Carnivore (a meat-eating dinosaur)

Omnivore (a plant- and meat-eating dinosaur)

T = Triassic period

J = Jurassic period

C = Cretaceous period

AFROVENATOR
say *af-ro-vee-nay-tor*
"African hunter"
Type theropod
L 30 feet ***H*** 10 feet ***W*** 3,000 pounds

AGUSTINIA
say *ah-gus-tin-ee-ah*
"for Agustin"
Type sauropod
L 50 feet ***H*** 15 feet ***W*** 20,000 pounds

ALLOSAURUS
say *al-oh-saw-russ*
"different lizard"
Type theropod
L 40 feet ***H*** 15 feet ***W*** 6,600 pounds

ANKYLOSAURUS
say *an-key-low-saw-rus*
"fused lizard"
Type ankylosaur
L 20 feet ***H*** 9 feet ***W*** 8,000 pounds

ARGENTINOSAURUS
say *are-jen-teen-owe-saw-rus*
"silver lizard"
Type sauropod
L 130 feet ***H*** 35 feet ***W*** 160,000 pounds

BARYONYX
say *ba-ree-on-ix*
"heavy claw"
Type theropod
L 32 feet ***H*** 15 feet ***W*** 4,400 pounds

BRACHIOSAURUS
say *brack-ee-oh-saw-rus*
"arm lizard"
Type sauropod
L 80 feet ***H*** 42 feet ***W*** 155,000 pounds

CERATOSAURUS
say *see-rat-oh-saw-rus*
"horned lizard"
Type ceratosaur
L 18 feet ***H*** 10 feet ***W*** 3,000 pounds

CHIALINGOSAURUS
say *chee-ah-ling-oh-saw-rus*
"Chialing lizard"
Type stegosaur
L 13 feet ***H*** 5 feet ***W*** 500 pounds

COELOPHYSIS
say *see-low-fy-sis*
"hollow form"
Type theropod
L 10 feet ***H*** 3 feet ***W*** 100 pounds

COMPSOGNATHUS
say *comp-sog-nay-thus*
"pretty jaw"
Type theropod
L 28 inches ***H*** 10 inches ***W*** 6 pounds

DEINOCHEIRUS
say *dine-oh-kir-us*
"terrible hand"
Type ornithomimosaur
L 23–38 feet ***H*** 10 feet ***W*** 20,000 pounds

DEINONYCHUS
say *die-non-i-kuss*
"terrible claw"
Type dromeosaur
L 10 feet ***H*** 5 feet ***W*** 175 pounds

DIPLODOCUS
say *dee-plod-oh-cus*
"double-beam"
Type sauropod
L 90 feet ***H*** 16 feet ***W*** 27,000 pounds

DROMICEIOMIMUS
say *droh-mee-see-oh-my-mus*
"emu mimic"
Type ornithomimosaur
L 12 feet ***H*** 6 feet ***W*** 250 pounds

EUOPLOCEPHALUS
say *you-oh-plo-sef-ah-lus*
"well-armored head"
Type ankylosaur
L 23 feet ***H*** 8 feet ***W*** 4,000 pounds

FRUITADENS
say *fruit-ah-denz*
"fruita tooth"
Type heterodontosaur
L 28 inches ***H*** 12 inches ***W*** 2 pounds

GRYPOSAURUS
say *grip-oh-saw-us*
"hook-nosed lizard"
Type hadrosaur
L 30 feet ***H*** 12–14 feet ***W*** 6,000 pounds

IGUANODON
say *ig-wah-no-don*
"iguana tooth"
Type iguanodont
L 30 feet ***H*** 12 feet ***W*** 9,900 pounds

MAMENCHISAURUS
say *mah-men-chee-saw-rus*
"mamen lizard"
Type sauropod
L 75 feet ***H*** 30 feet ***W*** 30,000 pounds

MASSOSPONDYLUS
say *mass-oh-spon-dye-luss*
"massive vertebra"
Type prosauropod
L 16 feet ***H*** 6 feet ***W*** 300 pounds

Nomingia
say *no-ming-ee-uh*
"Nomingiin" (part of the Gobi desert)
Type oviraptor
L 6 feet ***H*** 2½ feet ***W*** 70 pounds

Oviraptor
say *ov-ee-rap-tor*
"egg thief"
Type theropod
L 8 feet ***H*** 3 feet ***W*** 75 pounds

Protoceratops
say *pro-toe-sair-ah-tops*
"first horned face"
Type ceratopsian
L 8 feet ***H*** 3 feet ***W*** 900 pounds

Scipionyx
say *sip-ee-on-ix*
"scipio's claw"
Type theropod
L 6 feet ***H*** 2½ feet ***W*** 25 pounds

Scutellosaurus
say *skoo-tel-o-saw-us*
"little shield lizard"
Type thyreophora
L 4 feet ***H*** 18 inches ***W*** 25 pounds

Seismosaurus
say *size-mow-saw-rus*
"earthquake lizard"
Type sauropod
L 130 feet ***H*** 18 feet ***W*** 66,000 pounds

Spinosaurus
say *spy-no-saw-rus*
"spiny lizard"
Type spinosaur
L 60 feet ***H*** 22 feet ***W*** 20,000 pounds

Stegosaurus
say *steg-oh-saw-rus*
"roofed lizard"
Type stegosaur
L 30 feet ***H*** 9 feet ***W*** 6,000 pounds

Styracosaurus
say *sty-rak-o-saw-us*
"spiked lizard"
Type ceratopsian
L 18 feet ***H*** 6 feet ***W*** 6,500 pounds

Triceratops
say *tyr-seer-ah-tops*
"three horned face"
Type ceratopsian
L 30 feet ***H*** 10 feet ***W*** 22,000 pounds

Tyrannosaurus
say *tie-ran-oh-saw-rus*
"tyrant lizard king"
Type tyrannosaur
L 40 feet ***H*** 18 feet ***W*** 14,000 pounds

Velociraptor
say *vel-oh-see-rap-tor*
"speedy thief"
Type theropod
L 6 feet ***H*** 3 feet ***W*** 65 pounds

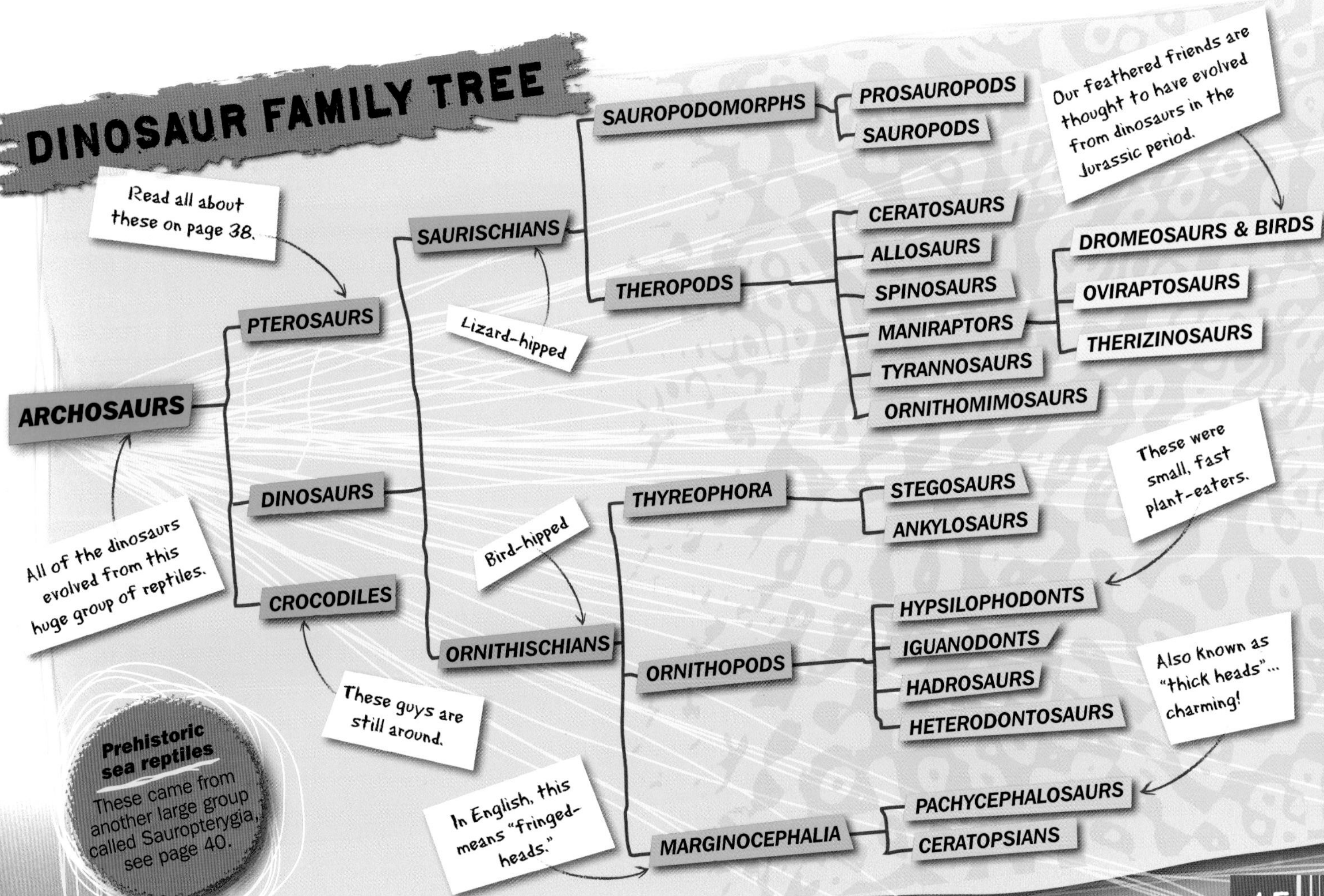

DINOSAURS INDEX

Bold numbers refer to main entries; numbers in *italic* refer to the illustrations

ACKNOWLEDGMENTS

COVER (dp) © zsollere – Fotolia.com, (r) Leonardo Meschini Advocate Art **2** (b) © Ralf Kraft – Fotolia.com; **2–3** © Robert King – Fotolia.com; **3** (t) © Fabian Kerbusch – iStock.com; **4** (b/l) © Sergey Drozdov – Fotolia.com; **5** (t/r) © Klaus Nilkens – iStock.com; **6** Mark Garlick/Science Photo Library; **6–7** © Metin Tolun – Fotolia.com; **7** (sp) © Alwyn Cooper – iStock.com, (t/l) © Bill May – iStock.com, (r) © Todd Harrison – iStock.com; **8** (l) © Ericos – Fotolia.com, (r) © Olga Orehkova-Sokolova – Fotolia.com; **8–9** (b) © zobeedy – Fotolia.com; **9** (t) © Metin Tolun – Fotolia.com, (t/r) Laurie O'keefe/Science Photo Library, (l) © Olga Orehkova-Sokolova – Fotolia.com, (r) © Ericos – Fotolia.com; **10** (t/l) © Didier Dutheil/Sygma/Corbis, (r) Photo courtesy of Charlie and Florence Magovern; **10–11** (c) © Metin Tolun – Fotolia.com; **11** (t/r) Reuters/STR New, (t) © Bill May – iStock.com, (b/r) © Didier Dutheil/Sygma/Corbis; **12** (b/l) Mikkel Juul Jensen/Bonnier Publications/Science Photo Library, (c) © Robert King – Fotolia.com, (t) © Fabian Kerbusch – iStock.com, (t/r) Eightfish; **13** (t) © Fabian Kerbusch – iStock.com, (t/r) © greenmedia – Fotolia.com, (c/r) © LianeM – Fotolia.com, (r) © Duey – Fotolia.com, (b/r) Reuters/Sergio Moraes, (sp) © Czardases – Fotolia.com; **14–15** Leonardo Meschini Advocate Art; **16** (sp) Roger Harris/Science Photo Library **17** (b/l) © Metin Tolun – Fotolia.com, (b/cl) © Bill May – iStock.com, (t) Christian Jegou Publiphoto Diffusion/Science Photo Library, (b) Reuters/STR New; **18** (t) De Agostini/Getty Images, (t/l) © Paul Moore – Fotolia.com, (b) © Metin Tolun – Fotolia.com, (b/r) Highlights for Children (OSF)/www.photolibrary.com; **18–19** (sp) © Ivan Bliznetsov – iStock.com, (r, l) © Steven van Soldt – iStock.com; **19** (t) Photoshot, (t/l) © Joonarkan – Fotolia.com, (c) © Sabina – Fotolia.com, (b) De Agostini/Getty Images; **20–21** Leonardo Meschini Advocate Art; **21** (t/r) © Olga Orehkova-Sokolova – Fotolia.com; **22–23** Leonardo Meschini Advocate Art; **24** (sp) Colin Keates; **25** (t/l) © Michael S. Yamashita/Corbis, (t/r) Ken Lucas, (b) Dea Picture Library; **26** (c) © Ralf Kraft – Fotolia.com (b/l, t/r) © Serhiy Zavalnyuk – iStock.com, (b/r) © Little sisters – Fotolia.com; **26–27** © klikk – Fotolia.com; **27** (t/l) © Little sisters – Fotolia.com, (t/r) © Olga Orehkova-Sokolova – Fotolia.com, (b) Peter Menzel/Science Photo Library; **28–29** Leonardo Meschini Advocate Art; **30** (b/c) Leonardo Meschini Advocate Art, (b) © Metin Tolun – Fotolia.com; **30–31** © Petya Petrova – Fotolia.com; **31** (t/l) Jeffrey L. Osborn, (t, b) © Metin Tolun – Fotolia.com, (b/r) Joe Tucciarone/Science Photo Library; **32** (t/r) Nigel Tisdall/Rex Features; **32–33** (dp) © Louie Psihoyos/Science Faction/Corbis; **33** (r) Christian Darkin/Science Photo Library; **34** (l) © Louie Psihoyos/Science Faction/Corbis, (b/l, b/r) © zobeedy – Fotolia.com, (b/c) © N & B – Fotolia.com; **34–35** Leonardo Meschini Advocate Art; **35** (b/l) © Pawel Nowik – Fotolia.com, (b/c) © N & B – Fotolia.com, (b/cr) © a_elmo – Fotolia.com, (b/r) © zobeedy – Fotolia.com; **36** (t) © Louie Psihoyos/Science Faction/Corbis, (b/r) © Chris Hepburn – iStock.com; **36–37** (dp) © Vladimir Wrangel – Fotolia.com; **37** (t/r) Reuters/Ho New, (b) © Louie Psihoyos/Corbis; **38** (t/l) © Gijs Bekenkamp – iStock.com; **38–39** Jaime Chirinos/Science Photo Library; **39** (t/l) Joe Tucciarone/Science Photo Library, (t) © Hypergon – iStock.com, (t/r) Richard Bizley/Science Photo Library; **40** (c) Getty Images, (b) search4dinosaurs.com; **41** Reuters/Ho New; **42** (b/r) © Darren Hendley – iStock.com, (c/r) © nikzad khaledi – iStock.com, (t/l) D. Van Ravenswaay/Science Photo Library, (t) Mauricio Anton/Science Photo Library; **43** Mark Garlick/Science Photo Library

Key: t = top, b = bottom, c = center, l = left, r = right, sp = single page, dp = double page, bgd = background

All other photos are from Ripley's Entertainment Inc. All other artwork by Rocket Design (East Anglia) Ltd.

Every attempt has been made to acknowledge correctly and contact copyright holders and we apologize in advance for any unintentional errors or omissions, which will be corrected in future editions.

TWISTS

a Jim Pattison Company

Written by Camilla de la Bedoyere
Consultant Barbara Taylor

Publisher Anne Marshall

Managing Editor Rebecca Miles
Picture Researcher James Proud
Editors Lisa Regan, Rosie Alexander
Assistant Editor Amy Harrison
Proofreader Judy Barratt
Indexer Hilary Bird

Art Director Sam South
Design Rocket Design (East Anglia) Ltd
Reprographics Stephan Davis

www.ripleybooks.com

CONTENTS!

PAGE 9

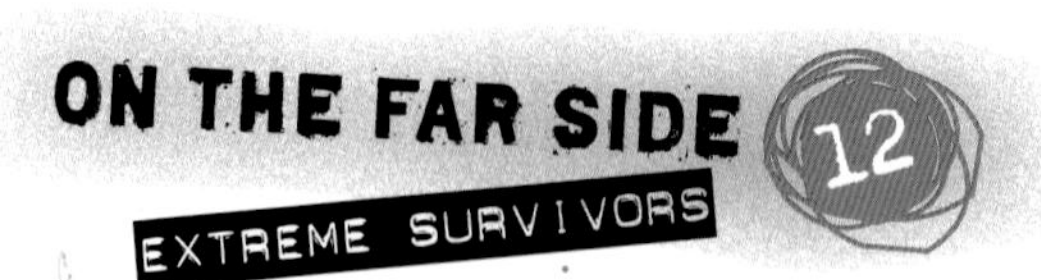

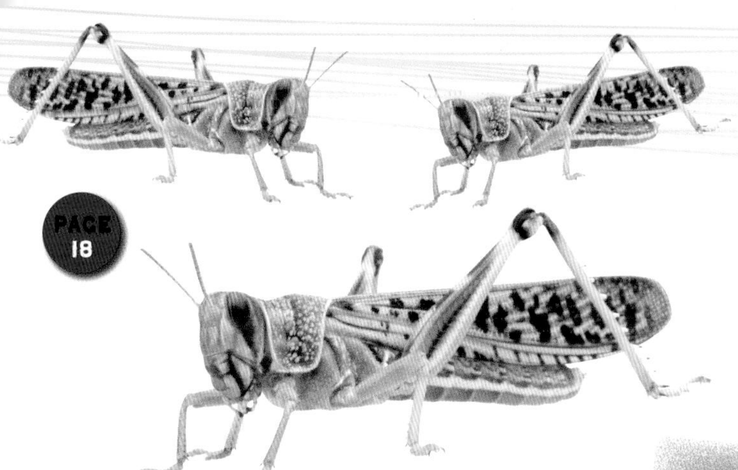
PAGE 18

PAGE 43

ALL CREATURES GREAT AND SMALL

WORLDWIDE WONDERS

Aren't animals amazing? From tiny terrors to gentle giants, vicious predators to graceful grazers, our planet is home to over one million different species. Each one of these species has an important role to play in the way the world works. That's why it's so vital that we consider how our lifestyles affect the homes and habitats of every living creature today.

WHAT'S INSIDE YOUR BOOK?

This book will open your eyes to the truly astonishing, the fearsomely frightening, and even the fantastically freakish members of the animal kingdom. Find out more about ocean dwellers, microscopic marvels, and endangered creatures, with Ripley's fascinating facts and amazing "Believe It or Not!" stories from around the world. Come on—read all about it!

Only male lions have a mane of long hair around their face. The males defend the pride (group) of lions and their territory, but the females are in charge of hunting and bringing home supper for the whole pride.

30

KEY FACTS

A pride may cover up to 100 square miles as its territory.

Lions learn to hunt when they are about a year old.

A lion has a claw at the back of its leg, which it sometimes uses to pick leftovers from its teeth!

The back teeth are used for cutting meat (rather than grinding food, like many other animals).

TWISTS

Do the twist

This book is packed with incredible creatures. It will teach you amazing things about wild animals, but like all Twists books, it shines a spotlight on things that are unbelievable but true. Turn the pages and find out more...

Twists are all about Believe It or Not: amazing facts, feats, and things that will make you go "Wow!".

The animal kingdom is full of creatures that sound like they're made up, but they're totally for real. Like this two-headed turtle, which has two heads, a pair of front feet on each side, one pair of back legs, and one tail. It's actually conjoined twins, and is on display in an aquarium in Pennsylvania.

Found a new word? Big word alerts will explain it for you.

FAMILY MATTERS

GETTING TOGETHER

The multi-colored peacock is a bird that dresses to impress. He can fan out his tail, in an eye-opening display of shimmering colors and stunning patterns.

It's an ingenious tactic; a show-off with perfect plumage is more likely to attract the attention of the watching peahens. The females admire bright colors and large "eyespots" in the feathers—and the more eyespots the better! Once a female has chosen her favorite male she will mate with him, and soon starts laying eggs. The most marvelous males win over a number of females to mate with, while shabby-looking peacocks remain alone.

BIG WORD ALERT

REPRODUCTION
The way that an animal has young is called reproduction. Some animals can have young all by themselves, but it's more common to have two parents: a male and a female.

LIFE STORIES

The story of how an animal lives, from birth to death, is a life-cyc…

If an animal can find a healthy and strong mate it is more likely to … youngsters that will survive. Some animals make a big effort to impre… those they fancy—to show how fit they are. This is called a courtship.

Mammals are animals that give birth to live young and feed them with milk. Usually it's the mom who provides the milk, but in the job-shar… world of Dayak fruit bats, it's a job for the dads too!

The Virginia opossum is the USA's only naturally occurring marsupial.

After about 100 days, the babies climb onto their mom's back to hitch a ride.

The newborns crawl straight into their mother's pouch to grow.

An opossum mom usually has 13 babies at once.

You said we were friends!
During mating, a female praying mantis usually gets the munchies and bites off her partner's head!

twist it!

TRUE LOVE

Sea horses are romantic, dancing for each other every day during the mating period. The female lays her eggs inside a special pouch on the male's body, and he takes care of them until they hatch.

Female rhinos spray smelly urine, and males will fight each other, sometimes to the death, to mate with them.

Amphibians, such as frogs and toads, have to lay their eggs in water. Snakes and lizards are reptiles and lay their eggs on land.

A queen white ant, or termite, lays 30,000 eggs a day!

DADDY DAY-CARE

Male jawfish protect their eggs by keeping them inside their enormous mouths. Without their fatherly care, chances are that most of the eggs would be eaten before ever hatching.

31

FASCINATING FACT!

Look for the Ripley R to find out even more than you knew before!

Learn fab fast facts to go with the cool pictures.

Don't forget to look out for the "twist it!" column on some pages. Twist the book to find out more fast facts about amazing animals.

ARMED AND DANGEROUS

PREDATORS

If you are fitted out with killer claws, razor-sharp teeth, or toxic venom you could be a perfect predator—an animal that hunts to eat.

Which predator would you place at the top of a league for mean, keen, killing machines? Sharks are a favorite for first place—after all, they've been prowling the oceans for around 400 million years. That means they were slicing through flesh 200 million years before the dinosaurs started plodding around on land! So are these hungry hunters the world's top predators? Since people kill around 100 million sharks every year—driving many types to the edge of extinction—that top spot might actually belong to us shame-faced humans.

The alligator snapping turtle catches fish when they seize its tongue, which they mistake for a worm.

BIG WORD ALERT

PREDATORS Animals that kill and eat other animals. The animals they kill are called prey.

Tiger sharks attack almost anything, including people. One was found with cans, tires, wood, half a dead dog, and a tom-tom drum in its belly!

Open wide

The Great White shark attacks ferociously, then retreats, letting the damaged prey grow weaker. Then it returns to finish it off. Each year, 50 to 100 serious shark attacks are reported, with an average of less than ten deaths.

THE FROG THAT FOUGHT BACK!

When this little tree frog got attacked by a cat-eyed snake he decided he wasn't going to give up without a fight. He grabbed hold of the snake's neck, and the predator and prey were still locked in mortal combat three hours later!

Just one bite!

In 1963, spearfishing champion Rodney Fox was attacked by a Great White shark in the ocean off Aldinga Beach, Australia. He had been virtually bitten in half and required 462 stitches. Less than three months later, however, he was back in the water, carrying a reminder of the attack embedded in his hand: a Great White tooth.

FASCINATING FACT! FASCINATING FACT!

Knockout!

Mantis shrimps are a knockout! These crustaceans have the fastest and most powerful punch in the animal kingdom. They can pound their prey with a force of 1,000 newtons—that's as deadly as a rifle bullet, and strong enough to smash glass. The shrimp's weapons are a pair of club-shaped legs that are tucked away under its head, until the time comes to lash out at a super-ballistic speed of up to 790 feet/second!

A shrimp's weapons of smash destruction are folded under its head until it's time for lunch.

TINY TERROR

When it is worried, the blue-ringed octopus buzzes with color. Its blue ring markings pulse brightly and its brown skin turns a vivid yellow. It measures only about 8 inches from armtip to armtip, but it has a deadly bite, which contains enough venom to kill at least seven people. In 1967, a man paddling in an Australian rock pool lived for just 90 minutes after being bitten.

TAKE A DIVE

DEEP DWELLERS

Oceans teem with animal life, from crystal-clear waters around coral reefs, to their darkest, inky depths. This may be where life on Earth began—simple creatures were burrowing in the slime of the ocean floor an unbelievable one billion years ago!

Oceans and seas are a mighty food store, and home to all sorts of creatures, from enormous blue whales with an average length of 90 feet, to tiny rotifers—each one smaller than a grain of salt. From the shallow shore to the deep ocean trenches, more than 6 miles beneath the surface, animals are crawling, slithering, tunneling, swimming, floating, and drifting.

When the tiny male anglerfish mates, he grabs the larger female with his mouth, hangs on, and gradually fuses (joins) with her body.

In the vast, black ocean depths it can take time to find a breeding partner. The male deep-sea anglerfish becomes a part of the female. He shares her food via her blood supply, and in return fertilizes her eggs.

Most of the male body disintegrates (his eyes, nostrils, everything) apart from what is needed to fertilize the female's eggs. Once this takes place, the male can never leave.

BIG WORD ALERT

PHYTOPLANKTON

The oceans are packed with phytoplankton (say: fie-toe-plank-ton). These mini plants get energy from sunlight, and are the favorite food of billions of animals.

WAY DOWN

Fish were the first animals with backbones to evolve on Earth and there are more than 30,000 species, or different types, of fish. Most of them live in the oceans or seas.

A shark's skeleton isn't made of bone, it's made of cartilage. That's the soft stuff you have holding your nose together. There are around 500 species of shark, of which only about 40 occasionally attack people.

Clownfish seek safety in the stinging tentacles of sea-anemones. The fish are immune to the stings, and clean the anemone in return for a safe place to live.

If you spot puffer fish on a menu, don't order it! Although these fish are sometimes served in Japanese restaurants, they contain enough poison to kill a person in 20 minutes. Chefs have to train for years to learn how to remove all the deadly body parts. Would you risk it?

Coral reefs are ocean wildlife hotspots. They are formed from living creatures, called coral polyps, and are home to thousands of other types of water species. Many coral reefs are dying, due to pollution and human activity.

TWIST IT!

This red handfish looks grumpy! Maybe that's because he has to get around by walking on his "hands," which are really just fins.

Many ocean-going creatures crunch on krill. These little animals swim in giant groups called swarms.

Oceans and seas are salty, but rivers and lakes have much less salt in the water. Animals usually live in one or the other habitat, but rarely both.

Ripley's Believe It or Not!®

Slithering sea slugs lost their shells millions of years ago. They don't need them, because these soft-bodied creatures have toxins (poisons) and stinging cells in their skin. Their bright colors are a bold signal to keep clear, or prepare for pain!

Most animals that live in the seas and oceans are able to take oxygen from the water. Don't try this in the bathtub: we're equipped with air-breathing lungs, not gills.

YIKES!

Deep in the oceans, where sunlight never reaches, there's a small army of weird creatures. Deep-water fish, such as this vicious viperfish, usually have dark bodies, huge mouths and hundreds of light organs called photophores. These are parts of the body that can actually make light, helping the fish to find food in the murky depths. The viperfish's teeth protrude far beyond its mouth and eyes, giving it the longest teeth of any animal (in proportion to its head). If your teeth were this big, they would stick out a ridiculous 12 inches!

If you were an animal, would you choose to crawl like a caterpillar or fly like a moth? Flying wins every time—can you imagine the thrill of swooping and soaring through the air?

Only birds, bats, and insects use their own mighty muscle power to truly fly. That little problem hasn't put off other creatures, such as flying squirrels and frogs, from taking a brave leap and trusting the wind to carry them along. Gliding is great if you're lazy, but animals that soar through the air can't always control how they travel, and where they end up. So it's fingers crossed for a soft landing!

Eagle-eyed ospreys soar over water looking for fish. They plunge, feet first, and grab their prey with talons that are covered in slippery-fish gripping spikes. They can even close their nostrils when they dive, so they don't get water up their nose.

KEY FACTS

- Flying can be a great way to get beyond the reach of predators. Plus, while you're flying past that tree, you might just spot some juicy fruits to eat too...
- ...which is just as well, because flying is hard work. It takes a great deal of energy—flying animals have big appetites.
- A bird's flapping wings create an up-force, which lifts the animal into the sky.

A HEAD FOR HEIGHTS

FLYERS

It flies, it hums, and it sips nectar. Is it a hummingbird? No, this is a hummingbird hawk moth. When it flies, this insect's orange hindwings beat so fast they look like flickering flames, giving the impression that the moth is on fire.

Hummingbirds have trough-shaped tongues and long, skinny beaks. They work like a drinking straw—perfect for sipping sweet nectar and the occasional insect, too.

FASCINATING FACT

The heart of a ruby-throated hummingbird beats around 600 times a minute.

The hummingbird has the biggest heart and wings in proportion to body size of all warm-blooded animals!

twist it!

FLY BY

Want to know the funny thing about flying lemurs? They can't really fly, and aren't really lemurs! These furry mammals live in Southeast Asia and have kite-shaped membranes of skin stretched between their limbs. They leap off trees, spread out the skin, and glide for up to 450 feet.

It's almost impossible to swat a fly—they move quickly, have great eyesight that allows them to see in virtually every direction, and can sense the air moving in front of your hand long before it reaches them.

When a tropical two-wing flying fish needs to escape a predatory dolphin it flaps its enormous fins to gain liftoff, and sails out of the water and through the air for up to 40 seconds.

Bats are the only mammals that can fly, rather than glide. Their wings are made from double layers of skin that stretch from fingers to ankles.

WOW!

Wallace's flying frog is an amphibian with an ambition to fly! It may not have wings, but this animal has got wide webbed feet and skin flaps that catch the air. When a frog jumps from a tree it can glide for up to 50 feet.

>> HIGH-FLYERS >>

- Some bats chase moths to heights of 10,000 feet.
- Alpine choughs (a type of bird) fly at 30,000 feet in the Himalayas.
- Queen of Spain Fritillary butterflies have been found at 9,000 feet.

ON THE FAR SIDE

EXTREME SURVIVORS

Animals have to cope with extremes of temperature and all sorts of difficult conditions. If you're thirsty, you get a glass of water. If you're cold, you put on more clothes. It's all about controlling what's going on inside, and outside, so your body can reach maximum performance levels. And that's what animals do, too.

FISH ON THE ROCKS

The blood of an icefish contains chemical antifreeze, which stops it from turning solid in the chilly waters of the Antarctic.

warm wallow

Japanese macaques make the most of the cold weather by enjoying a dip in the warm waters of a hot spring. They have even been known to make and throw snowballs, rolling them along the ground to get bigger and better ones!

HABITAT
The place an animal lives. Some animals have evolved to be able to live in extreme habitats.

KEY FACTS

- It's worth being an extreme survivor if you can find safety or food in a place where few other animals venture.
- Animals living in very hot, cold, dry, or wet places often need super-adapted body parts.

BIG BULLY!

Frogs like it damp, so when there is no rain, large African bullfrogs bury themselves underground. They can survive for several years, wrapped in a cocoon so they don't dry out.

This African frog has seized its prey—a small mouse!

EXTREMES!

Less than ½ inch of rain falls in the Namibian Desert every year. Desert adders living there don't drink water: they get all they need from the lizards they eat.

Some animals sleep their way through the worst weather of winter. Little Siberian birch mice hibernate for up to eight months of the year.

Black grouse spend up to 95 percent of the winter hidden deep in snow burrows. The only time they emerge is to have a snack!

Musk oxen have been around since the Ice Age, and they still use thick woolen coats to keep them warm in Alaska. Their fur reaches to the ground, and is the longest growing hair of any animal.

twist it!

WHO'S THE COLDEST?

- Arctic foxes can survive at −22°F if well fed.
- Snow buntings nest nearer to the North Pole than any other bird.
- Ptarmigans can survive sub-zero temperatures for six weeks.
- Himalayan yaks survive at a height of 20,000 feet on ice-fields.

Little baby ears are perfect for keeping in body heat.

Two layers of thick fur help to keep out the cold.

You won't see a polar bear putting on a coat! This extreme survivor has got a body that can cope with sub-zero temperatures. In fact, polar bears get too hot sometimes, and roll around in the snow to chill out! They are the largest predators on land.

Who's the biggest?

TALLEST GIRAFFE
19 feet 8 inches (in height)

BIGGEST DINOSAUR
Argentinosaurus
98 feet (in length)

LARGEST ON LAND
African elephant
35 feet (from trunk to tail)

BIGGEST EVER BLUE WHALE
110 feet (in length)

This enormous individual was a real giant amongst elephants. He was an African bush elephant and was shot in Angola in 1974. He measured 13 feet 8 inches to the shoulder and was thought to weigh 13.5 tons, which makes him about twice the length and weight of an average bull elephant. The elephant was stuffed and you can now see him in the Smithsonian Museum of Natural History, Washington DC, USA.

HORN OF PLENTY

Lurch, an African Watusi steer, has horns that are 7 feet 6 inches across and 38 inches around... and they're still growing! His parents have perfectly normal horns.

Tallest animal!

The giraffe has a tongue almost 20 inches in length!

MEGA!

Millipedes have more legs than any other creature, but they don't actually have 1,000 of them. The most ever counted on one millipede was 750 legs.

Gaboon vipers have hollow teeth that pump venom into their victim. They have the longest fangs of any snake and one bite contains enough venom to kill ten people.

For its size, the rhino beetle is the strongest animal on the planet, and can move an object 850 times its own weight!

The world's biggest earthworms can grow to 16½ feet long, and are as thick as your arm. Bootlace worms, found in coastal areas of Britain, can measure 180 feet!

Deep in the oceans, whales talk to each other using grunting and moaning sounds. Some of these sounds are the loudest animal noises ever recorded. They are about as loud as a rocket taking off!

twist it!

Spotted skunks stink...and that's official. They are the smelliest animals alive, and even perform headstands when they spray their foul liquids, to get the best results.

BIG, REALLY BIG!

A colossal squid is a giant in anyone's book. This one turned up in the nets of a fishing boat in the Ross Sea, near Antarctica. It was the first intact specimen ever seen, measured around 33 feet in length, and had eyeballs bigger than dinner plates. They probably gave this creature great vision deep underwater, where very little light can penetrate.

The stripe leg tarantula devours a tasty lizard. It is one of the largest spiders in the world and lives in the Amazon area of South America.

ACTUAL SIZE!

OVERSIZE JUMPER

This goliath frog must be hopping mad he got caught! These bulky amphibians live in West Africa and can measure 16 inches from nose to tail.

BLACK-OUT

Tiny tarsiers live in the rain forests of Southeast Asia. They spend most of their time scampering through trees, using their long, slender fingers to grip to branches. Tarsiers can turn their heads right around, to check what's going on behind them, and use their enormous eyes and excellent hearing to listen for prowling predators.

Little fennec foxes have enormous ears. They live in the desert and come out to hunt when the sun goes down. Their large ears help them to listen for prey, but they also help the foxes to lose heat during the boiling desert days.

A mole 6 inches long can dig a tunnel almost 230 feet long in a single night.

A solitary dingo (a species of Australian wild dog) can kill 50 sheep in one night.

Oilbirds spend their entire lives in darkness, inhabiting the caves of South America. They venture out at night to feed on fruit and find their way around using echolocation.

twist it!

A barn owl, hearing a mouse, can take off in half a second, fly 12½ feet per second, and adjust its talons to the size and shape of its prey—in the dark!

The barn owl catches more mice than 12 cats!

Watch this!

An owl's eyes take up about half of the space in its head.

WHOO'S THERE?

NOCTURNAL HUNTERS

When the sun slips down in the sky, stealthy stalkers begin to stir. Millions of animals, from wolves to wombats, join the wide-awake club and get active under the cover of night.

On the up side, night workers should be hard to see, so they might avoid being eaten. The downer is that lots of other wide-awakers have got crafty methods for seeking out prey at night.

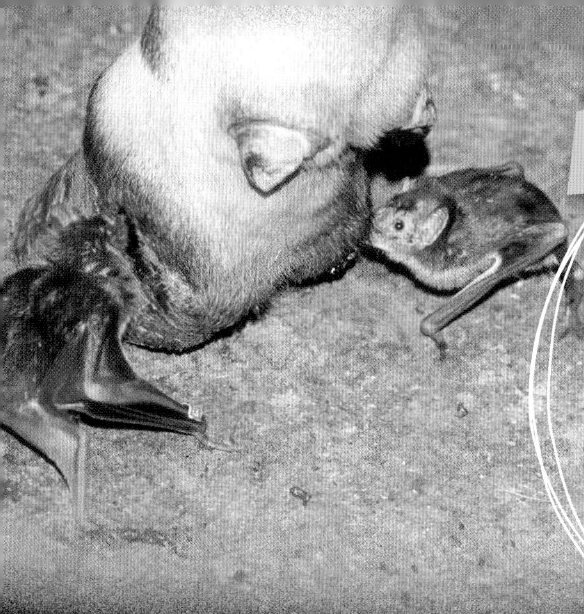

Suckers!

Blood-drinking vampire bats feed on other animals and, occasionally, humans too. Here they are feeding on a cow's foot, slicing through flesh, and sucking up the oozing blood. Chemicals in their spit stop the wound from healing.

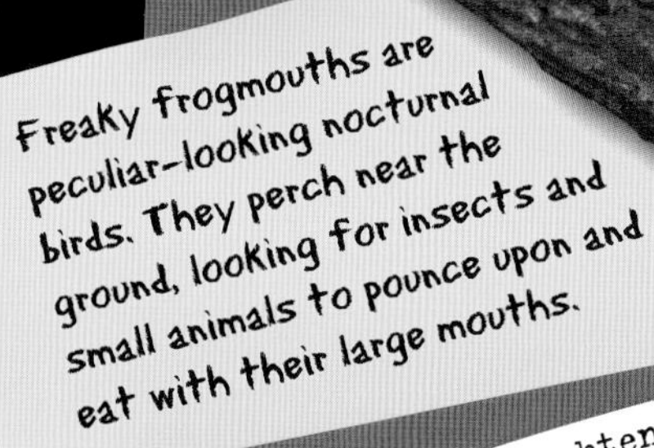

Freaky frogmouths are peculiar-looking nocturnal birds. They perch near the ground, looking for insects and small animals to pounce upon and eat with their large mouths.

If a frogmouth is frightened it clings to a tree, stays still, and pretends to be a broken branch!

Ouch!

Barn owls usually swallow their small prey whole. Creatures such as mice, birds, lizards, and frogs are eaten, feathers, bones, and all!

KEY FACTS

- Around half of all the animals that live on land are nocturnal. That means they head out and about at night, but sleep in the day.
- Nocturnal creatures often need super senses, so they can find their way around in the dark.
- Animals that live in hot places often stir at night, because it's easier to keep cool once the sun has set.

Ripley's Believe It or Not!® Night beast

A strange hairless animal was found dead outside Cuero, Texas, in August 2007. It was thought to be a chupacabra, a mythical nocturnal beast. The chupacabra gets its name (Spanish for goat-sucker) from its habit of attacking and drinking the blood of livestock. Descriptions of a chupacabra vary: a hairless dog-like creature; a spiny reptile that hops and has red glowing eyes. As for this animal: some believed it was a fox with mange...or was it?

MIGHTY MUNCHERS

DINNER TIME

Feeling a bit empty inside? Are you hungry enough to eat 2,500 hamburgers? If you were a furry shrew, that's the same amount of food you'd have to find and eat every day of your life! Except it wouldn't be burgers you'd be eating, it would be nearly your own body weight in bugs, slugs, and grubs. Tasty!

YUK!

Spotted hyenas are the most powerful scavengers in the world with jaws and teeth that can exert enough pressure to smash rocks, and can crush, and then digest, bone, horn, hooves, and hides.

It's tough, but true: some animals need to eat all day long to stay alive. Consider a swarm of desert locusts: each insect weighs only 0.07 ounces, but when you've got 16,000,000,000 of them devouring any crops in their path, that's a jaw-dropping 35,000 tons of food every 24 hours.

really?

Big animals need lots of food. Most blue whales reach about 89 feet long and eat 2,200 pounds of krill every single day to survive. Krill are shrimp-like creatures, and each one is no bigger than your little finger!

Faddy diets are common in nature. Giant anteaters, for example, are fussy eaters that devour tens of thousands of ants and termites daily. They can't eat anything else. Vampire bats live on a diet of blood.

Some animals swallow food whole, others mash it with their teeth first. Flies, however, vomit burning juices on to their lunch before sucking it up like soup. Yum!

Ripley's Believe It or Not!®

One sandtiger shark in the "womb" kills and eats all of its brothers and sisters. A scientist was once dissecting a dead female sandtiger and had his finger bitten by the one surviving baby shark!

BIG WORD ALERT

OMNIVORE - Eats anything

HERBIVORE - Nature's vegetarians

CARNIVORE - Mighty meat eater

PISCIVORE - Loves a fish dinner

This 13-foot Burmese python bit off more than it could chew when it tried to swallow a 6-foot American alligator, whole. Both animals were found dead, floating in the water. Experts think the alligator was still alive when the snake swallowed it, snout-first, and that repeated kicks from its hind legs made a hole in the snake's stomach wall.

Snake's stomach.

Alligator's tail.

OPEN WIDE

Pets, like people, are getting bigger and unhealthier. Lack of exercise and over-feeding are causing pooches and pussycats to pile on the weight. The world's biggest domestic cats weigh as much as a five-year-old child!

The caterpillar of the polyphemus moth is a record-breaking mighty muncher. It eats 86,000 times its own birthweight in just 56 days. That's like a human baby eating 300 tons of food!

When Kyle, a small collie/Staffordshire bull terrier, got hungry, he swallowed a bread knife measuring 15 inches. Amazingly, Kyle survived his dangerous snack attack!

Dust mites make a meal from dead skin and hair. Millions can live in just an ounce of dust, causing asthma and other allergic symptoms.

When a Nile crocodile was killed in 1968, its stomach was found to contain the remains of a woman, two goats, and half a donkey!

twist it!

SPEED MERCHANTS

THE FASTEST

In the nasty world of nature there's one golden rule to staying alive: run for it! Whether you're chasing lunch, or on the menu yourself, speed is a vital survival skill. When a pronghorn antelope smells the hot breath of a coyote nearby, it springs into action. Within just a few seconds, these graceful grazers turn into power-houses that can reach breathtaking speeds of 42 mph for a mile, making them the world's fastest long-distance runners. How do humans compare? Even the world's speediest sprinter can manage only a measly 23 mph for ten seconds.

BIG WORD ALERT

ACCELERATE
When an animal increases its speed it accelerates.

A very flexible spine helps the cheetah make enormous strides.

Grippy claws dig in to accelerate.

Whoooosh!

Cheetahs are the fastest land animals over a short distance. They can achieve top speeds thanks to their light and muscular bodies. Their spine is incredibly flexible, which means these big cats can take enormous strides. Their claws grip the ground as they run, just like the spikes on a human sprinter's running shoes.

>> WHO'S THE FASTEST? >>

Peregrine falcon 124 mph

Sailfish 68 mph

Cheetah 60 mph

Pronghorn 42 mph

Speed freaks

<< Killer crabs

Ghost crabs are crusty crustaceans with ten legs, two of which are claws. They live by the ocean, and burrow into soft sand along the beach. At night, they come out to feed (this one is about to snack on a dead turtle) but the slightest disturbance will send them racing back to their tunnels. Ghost crabs run sideways very fast and can cover over 6 feet in just one second.

Living torpedoes >>

All penguins are clumsy waddlers on land, but watch them in the ocean and their funny-looking bodies are perfect for being propelled through water. They have torpedo-shaped bodies and wings like flippers that cut through water, reducing water resistance. Gentoo penguins of the Antarctic region are the fastest of all.

KEY FACTS

- Speed: it's brilliant for getting you out of trouble, but it takes a lot of energy, and a body that's built for rapid action.
- Being able to move fast is handy if you're a predator, as long as you can move quicker than your prey.
- If you belong to a speedy species you may find you become someone else's lunch when you can't move so fast. Most at risk are newborns, and injured or elderly animals.
- Speedy creatures need to eat plenty of food to replace all the energy they burn.

twist it!

A GOOD RUN

Three-toed sloths prefer slo-mo. It would take them an hour to walk 400 feet, if they could be bothered!

Animals on land can usually move more quickly, and easily, than animals under water. That's because water exerts a greater force (water resistance) than air. Peregrine falcons are the fastest animals of all when they fall into a dive because gravity helps them on their way.

Scientists at the University of Washington, USA, wanted to find out which reptile can move fastest, so they set up a racetrack! As the lizards raced they passed through light beams that triggered a timing device. The spiny-tailed iguana won the race, reaching an impressive 21 mph!

Despite their huge and bulky bodies, elephants can thunder along the African plains at speeds of 15 mph.

Man 23 mph

Iguana 21 mph

Elephant 15 mph

Sloth... 400 FEET per hour!

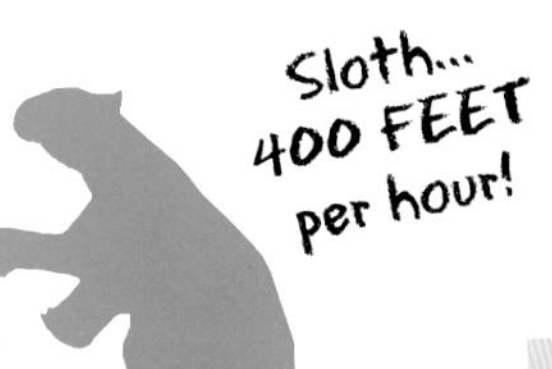

INCREDIBLE JOURNEYS

MIGRATION

Turtles have been swimming through the oceans for 220 million years. But it's hard to find any of them, because they are always on the move!

These shelled reptiles are a blast from the past, and have a weird creature feature: they go on marathon journeys. When a newly hatched female loggerhead turtle emerges from her egg, she is just 2 inches long. She wades into the sea and begins a lonely journey that will take up to ten years and cover nearly 10,000 miles. The adult turtle then returns to the same place where she hatched, to lay her own clutch of eggs.

DIAMOND RAYS

WHEN THOUSANDS OF GOLDEN RAYS SET OFF ON THEIR ANNUAL TRIP ALONG THE EASTERN COAST OF MEXICO, THEY TURN THE SEA INTO AN AWESOME DIAMOND-PATTERNED SPECTACLE. EACH FISH MEASURES UP TO 7 FEET ACROSS, AND SWIMS BY FLAPPING ITS ENORMOUS TRIANGULAR-SHAPED FINS LIKE WINGS.

WILDEBEEST VACATION

This is me!

Look mom, I can fly!

get off the line!
Sadly, my best friend Bob didn't make it.
Asking the lions for directions was not the best idea.
Ahhhh, the green, green, grass of home

COAST TRIP

Every year, 120 million red crabs crawl out of their burrows on Christmas Island and head to the coast. But this is no summertime spree... these brave crabs are marching off to mate. They have to make it past roads, railroads, and farms to reach the Indian Ocean.

BIG WORD ALERT

MIGRATION

A long journey is called a migration. These incredible trips usually happen at certain times of the year, and often following the same routes. Animals migrate to get to more food, or to find a better place to mate. Many migrations happen from places that are cold in winter to ones that are warm in summer. It's a bit like going on vacation.

When wily wildebeest travel they make a big deal of it, migrating for seven months in search of food. They follow the rains north, and can hear thunderstorms 20 miles away. They know that where there's rain there is juicy green grass. Yum!

MICROSCOPIC MARVELS

Get up close and personal with the hairy, scary side of nature. All you need is a microscope. All these creatures are magnified many times—scary!

KEY FACTS

- Microscopes magnify things, which means that they look bigger and you are able to see much more detail.
- Scientists can use Scanning Electron Microscopes (SEMs) to get brilliant pictures of tiny things. SEMs can magnify something 250,000 times!
- Without microscopes we wouldn't know much about bacteria, viruses, and other tiny living creatures.

Ant

Journey to OUTER SPACE!

No, it's not an alien, but this ant's cousins have been to space. Fifteen ant astronauts were sent into space so scientists could see how they coped with life there. The ants went crazy, digging tunnels!

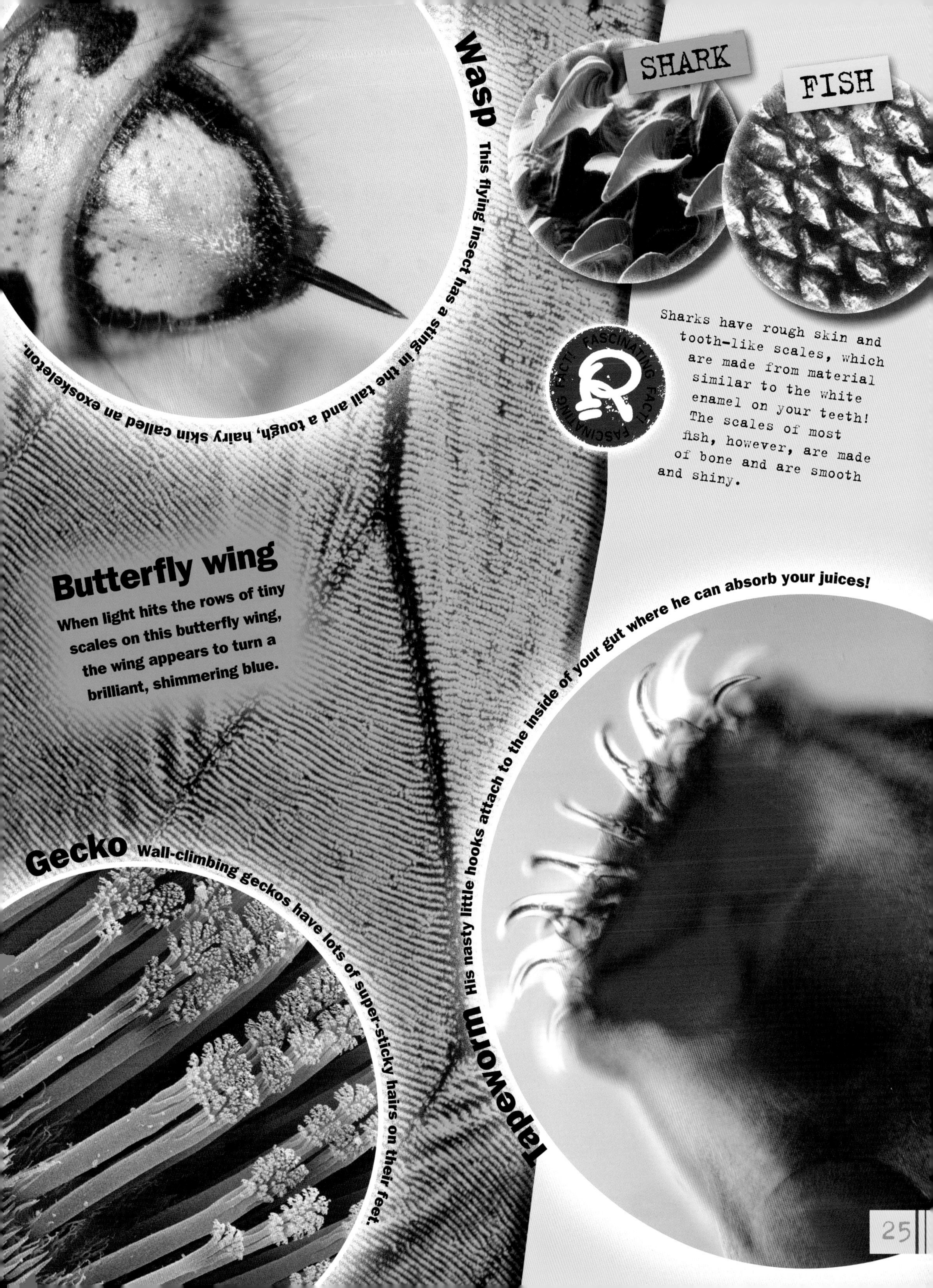

Wasp
This flying insect has a sting in the tail and a tough, hairy skin called an exoskeleton.

Sharks have rough skin and tooth-like scales, which are made from material similar to the white enamel on your teeth! The scales of most fish, however, are made of bone and are smooth and shiny.

Butterfly wing
When light hits the rows of tiny scales on this butterfly wing, the wing appears to turn a brilliant, shimmering blue.

Tapeworm
His nasty little hooks attach to the inside of your gut where he can absorb your juices!

Gecko
Wall-climbing geckos have lots of super-sticky hairs on their feet.

HOW CLEVER!

PROBLEM SOLVING

Imagine someone has put a wad of banknotes in a jar, and sealed it shut. If you can get the money out of the jar, it's yours. What would you do?

You'd quickly put your thinking cap on, of course! You use your brilliant brain to think up ways to tackle every problem you come across. That makes you one of the most intelligent animals on the planet, despite what your teachers might say! Maybe humans are the *most* intelligent species, but who knows? There are plenty of other clever creatures, and being a problem solver is a top survival skill in the competitive world of animals.

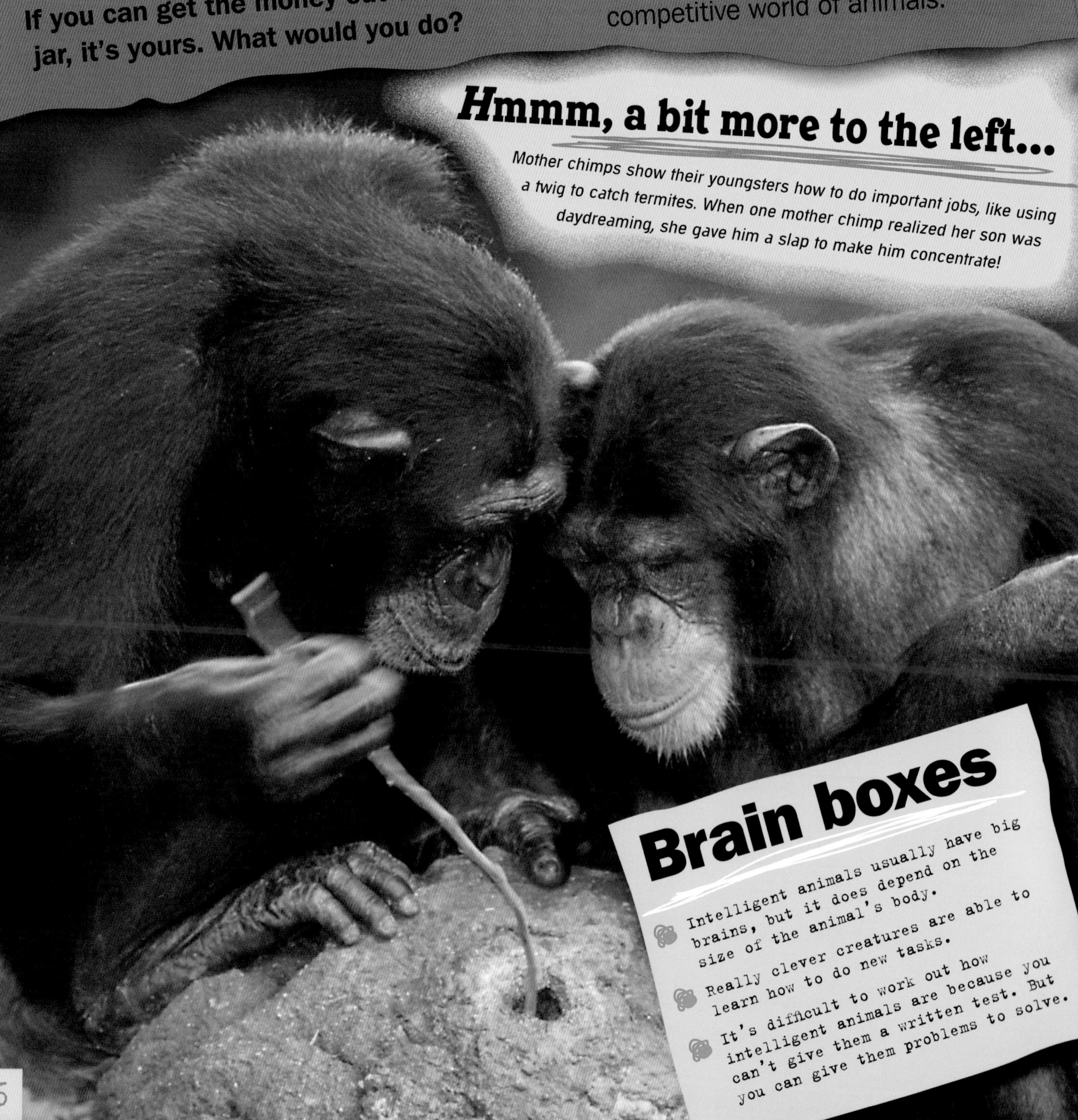

Hmmm, a bit more to the left...

Mother chimps show their youngsters how to do important jobs, like using a twig to catch termites. When one mother chimp realized her son was daydreaming, she gave him a slap to make him concentrate!

Brain boxes

- Intelligent animals usually have big brains, but it does depend on the size of the animal's body.
- Really clever creatures are able to learn how to do new tasks.
- It's difficult to work out how intelligent animals are because you can't give them a written test. But you can give them problems to solve.

HEY, I KNOW EWE

Sheep can recognize the faces of up to 50 other members of the flock!

twist it!

Are you left- or right-handed? It's thought that octopuses also have a favorite "arm," though, of course, they have eight to choose from. Scientists have given them toys such as blocks, balls, and puzzles to see whether there is a pattern to how they pick them up.

FISH FOOD

An archerfish shoots a jet of water at its insect prey to knock it down and gobble it up. Adult archerfish usually hit their target with the first shot, and this can be up to 5 feet away. If the prey is close to the water, however, the fish will leap out to grab it with its mouth.

Big baby!

This clever cuckoo has conned a mother wren into bringing it up in place of her own babies. Mom's the word!

BRAIN BOX

Orangutans sometimes use large leaves as umbrellas. They have even been seen to use leaves as napkins and "toilet paper."

Scientists have discovered that fish can tell the time, and they also have great memories, remembering things for up to three months.

Sea lions can remember tricks they learned ten years earlier. Trainers have taught sea lions that certain hand gestures have meaning, and they can understand a whole sentence of gestures, such as "fetch the large white ball."

Pigs have been trained to detect explosive mines in the field of war. Their trainers say they are better than dogs, because they are not only more intelligent, but also have a better sense of smell.

HIDE AND SEEK

More than 1.5 million types, or species, of animal have been found so far—but scientists are still looking for the other 28.5 million they think exist. Why can't these eagle-eyed researchers find them? Well, many creatures are either masters of disguise, or hide from view to survive!

It's a dog-eat-dog world out there and these clever defenders blend in with their surroundings to avoid becoming lunch. It's a cunning trick known as camouflage—and many animals, especially insects, are experts.

Camouflage isn't all about defense. Prowling predators, like striped tigers and spotted leopards, disappear among the dappled shadows of their forest homes. Becoming invisible is a handy trick when you're a hungry hunter!

CHAMELEON

Male panther chameleons live on the island of Madagascar and are famous for their fabulous displays of color. Their skin can turn from red to blue or green in seconds. A sudden flush of color impresses the ladies!

THORN BUGS

Cunningly disguised as sharp thorns, these female thorn bugs suck sap from a tree. Any keen-sighted bird that sees through the camouflage and takes a bite will quickly discover that these fancy fakers taste foul.

KEY FACTS

- Black, yellow, and red are nature's code for danger. Wearing stripes or spots in these colors can keep predators at bay, even if you're a totally harmless beastie.
- It doesn't matter how cleverly camouflaged you are if you stink. That's why smelly animals aren't usually camouflaged.
- Leaf-eating insects are so well disguised that there are maybe thousands of species that have never been spotted.

DANGER!

FASCINATING FACT!

They may be yellow, but they're not cowards! Frightened yellow-bellied toads flip onto their backs, showing brightly colored undersides. The yellow warns predators: "Danger: poison!"

Upside down!

Ripley's Believe It or Not!®

Chameleons use their color-changing skills to scare off love rivals rather than as camouflage. They can also change color when the temperature or light changes, or they are unwell.

Cuttlefish are eight-armed sea creatures that can send waves of shimmering color down their body, changing shades and patterns in seconds.

Stick insects stay still and make like a twig. If their cunning disguise isn't working, they drop all their legs off for maximum effect. Luckily, the legs grow back!

Sleepy sloths hang upside down in trees and snooze for 18 hours out of 24. Green plants grow in the sloths' fur, providing perfect camouflage in their rain forest homes.

LEAF INSECT

Leaf insects are one of nature's most extraordinary sights—if you ever get to see one, that is! This is Phyllium giganteum, the world's largest leaf insect, and it grows to more than 5 inches long.

where is it?

BARK MANTID

Don't challenge a bark mantid to a game of hide and go seek—unless you're happy to lose! They're quite common creatures in Australia, but you're only likely to see one if it's moving.

FAMILY MATTERS

GETTING TOGETHER

The multi-colored peacock is a bird that dresses to impress. He can fan out his tail, in an eye-opening display of shimmering colors and stunning patterns.

It's an ingenious tactic; a show-off with perfect plumage is more likely to attract the attention of the watching peahens. The females admire bright colors and large "eyespots" in the feathers—and the more eyespots the better! Once a female has chosen her favorite male she will mate with him, and soon starts laying eggs. The most marvelous males win over a number of females to mate with, while shabby-looking peacocks remain alone.

The Virginia opossum is the USA's only naturally occurring marsupial.

After about 100 days, the babies climb onto their mom's back to hitch a ride.

The newborns crawl straight into their mother's pouch to grow.

An opossum mom usually has 13 babies at once.

LIFE STORIES

The story of how an animal lives, from birth to death, is a life-cycle.

If an animal can find a healthy and strong mate it is more likely to have youngsters that will survive. Some animals make a big effort to impress those they fancy—to show how fit they are. This is called a courtship.

Mammals are animals that give birth to live young and feed them with milk. Usually it's the mom who provides the milk, but in the job-sharing world of Dayak fruit bats, it's a job for the dads too!

BIG WORD ALERT

REPRODUCTION
The way that an animal has young is called reproduction. Some animals can have young all by themselves, but it's more common to have two parents: a male and a female.

You said we were friends!

During mating, a female praying mantis usually gets the munchies and bites off her partner's head!

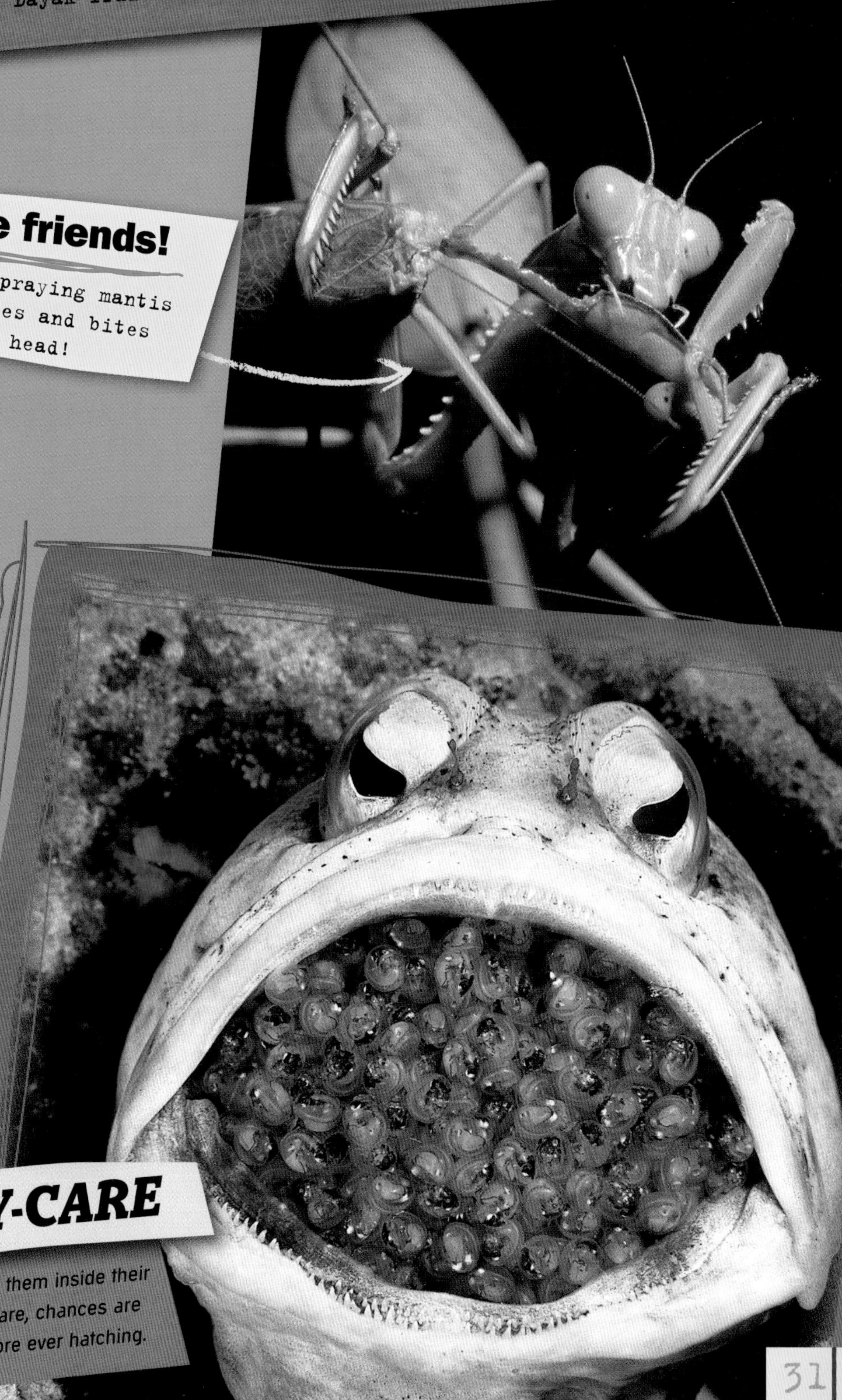

twist it!

TRUE LOVE

Sea horses are romantic, dancing for each other every day during the mating period. The female lays her eggs inside a special pouch on the male's body, and he takes care of them until they hatch.

Female rhinos spray smelly urine, and males will fight each other, sometimes to the death, to mate with them.

Amphibians, such as frogs and toads, have to lay their eggs in water. Snakes and lizards are reptiles and lay their eggs on land.

A queen white ant, or termite, lays 30,000 eggs a day!

DADDY DAY-CARE

Male jawfish protect their eggs by keeping them inside their enormous mouths. Without their fatherly care, chances are that most of the eggs would be eaten before ever hatching.

NATURAL BORN KILLERS

PROGRAMED TO KILL

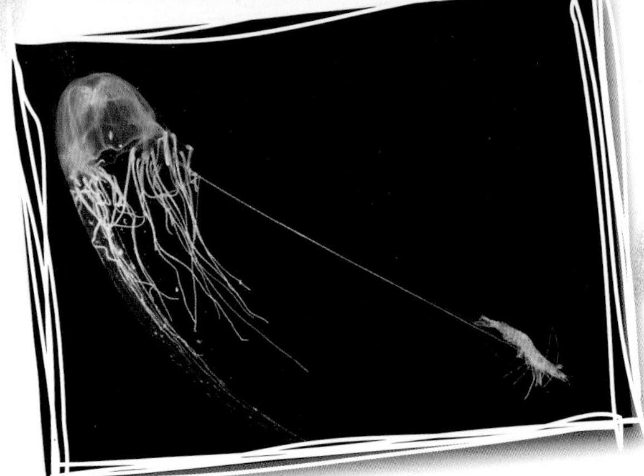

Imagine you are swimming in the beautiful clear waters of Australia when you feel something long and smooth glide over your leg. It's time to start counting: if you've been stung by a box jellyfish you've got about four minutes to live.

These animals, which are also known as sea wasps, are almost see-through and have long, trailing tentacles that are covered in rapid-fire stingers. If you haven't got any anti-venom tucked into your swimming suit you're in hot water! The poison from those stingers will give you excruciating pain, a burning feeling, and a one-way ticket to death.

Brown bears are dangerous, and do kill people!

BIG KILLERS

Brazilian wandering spider: there are more than 30 types of deadly spider, but this feisty beast has a bad temper and attacks anyone and anything.

Black mamba: this skinny snake is a super-speedy assassin. It lurks in trees or crevices before attacking and can slither faster than you can run! Its deadly venom acts quickly, but kills slowly and painfully.

Cape buffalo: this curly-horned bruiser is the bully of the African plains. Get in its way, and one of these big beasts will run you down like a tank at full speed.

Golden poison-dart frog: don't touch this little fella, or you'll croak! Its highly poisonous skin can cause instant death.

Plasmodium: this tiny creature lives in the spit of mosquitoes and causes the deadly disease malaria. Malaria is spread when mosquitoes bite people, and is responsible for around one million human deaths every year in Africa alone.

STAY SAFE

- Animals normally kill people only if they are very hungry or scared.
- Humans are in the most danger from deadly creatures when they move into those animals' natural habitats.
- The most dangerous animal on the planet is the human—that's us! Unlike most other animals, we are able to destroy entire environments, and totally wipe out other species.

The Brazilian wandering spider's venom causes unbelievable pain before death.

GRUESOME TALES

Ripley's Believe It or Not!®

One day, a Brazilian man found his six-year-old son in the jaws of an anaconda: that's an enormous South American snake. The poor boy had been nearly entirely swallowed. With no time to spare, the man picked up a wooden oar and smacked the snake with it, until it coughed the boy out. He was still alive!

Scott MacInnes is un-bear-ably unlucky. He lives in Alaska and has been attacked and savaged twice by brown bears. On the plus side, he did survive both attacks, despite major wounds.

Saltwater crocodiles don't kill people out of fear, but out of hunger. When a riverboat sank in Indonesia, in 1975, more than 40 passengers were set upon and eaten by saltwater crocs.

Ants are more deadly than they look. Bulldog ants and jumper ants inject painful acid into their prey, which can sometimes kill humans. There are rumors that columns of army ants and driver ants can climb all over a human victim, stinging and then eating them!

DEAD END

TWIST IT!

More people die from bee stings each year than from shark attacks or snake bites.

Gustave is a cold-blooded killer from Burundi. This giant African crocodile is rumored to have killed around 300 people.

Hippos kill more people in Africa than any other large animal. They are herbivores, but can attack humans to protect their calves and defend their territory.

Every year, 10,000 Indians lose their lives after being bitten by cobras.

One box jellyfish has enough venom to kill 60 people.

KILLING MACHINE

Saltwater crocodiles are the world's largest living reptiles, and unfortunately they've got big appetites, too. They are known as Australia's most dangerous animals.

SEE ME IN ACTION ON PAGE 23!

MEET THE UGLIES!

NATURE'S TOP 5

NAKED MOLE-RAT

Good looks don't matter to these burrowing mammals. They're nasty to look at, and nasty by nature: males kidnap youngsters from other colonies and keep them as slaves, forcing them to dig new tunnels.

1st

JUDGES' COMMENTS

It's put me totally off my breakfast!

JUDGES' COMMENTS

Unspeakably ugly—looks like my old math teacher!!

2nd

GIANT SUNFISH

A giant sunfish starts life as smallfry, but increases its weight 60 million times until adulthood—when it looks like a giant floating head and is the size of a car!

THORNY DEVIL

This Australian lizard is no shrinking violet. It feeds during the day, relying on camouflage and its armory of spines to keep it safe. A thorny devil can eat 2,500 ants in one meal!

JUDGES' COMMENTS

Good effort, we particularly like the big spiky boil on the back of the neck.

MARINE IGUANA

Ocean views and salty water don't suit any lizards—except the marine iguanas of the Galapagos Islands. These giant salt-covered sunbathers dive for food in the waters, or graze on seaweed in rocky pools nearby.

JUDGES' COMMENTS

Godzilla's ugly brother.

PROBOSCIS MONKEY

You've got to feel sorry for this fella. If he looks up too quickly his giant schnoz will flop back and smack him in the eyes! His pot belly and big nose are a hit with the ladies though.

JUDGES' COMMENTS

We felt the nice haircut really sets off the big flappy nose!

ANIMAL TALK COMMUNICATING

Dolphins whistle to each other, chimps bang tree trunks like drums, and a honeybee shakes its rear end in a weird wiggle dance. Animals may not be able to talk like us, but they can certainly get their messages across.

Communication is crucial. If you can talk to your friends you can warn them when a predator is nearby, tell them where they can find food, or declare your love! Stick a few bright and bold stripes or spots on your skin and you could be telling predators to stay away because you taste vile, or have vicious venom up your sleeve.

WHISTLE

Dolphins call to each other by whistling. Amazingly, a group of dolphins gives each dolphin a name—which has its own special whistle.

RUMBLE

WIGGLE

When a honeybee has found a good patch of flowers it flies back to the hive and starts dancing. By running up and down, and wiggling its body, the bee tells the others exactly where to find the flowers!

Elephants can communicate over many miles using very low rumbling sounds, which travel through the ground. Other elephants pick up these signals through their feet. This way, females can let adult males know they would be welcome to visit the herd!

YOU LOOKING AT ME?

SHRIEK

When a chimpanzee shrieks, he is telling the rest of the gang that he's found food. Chimps also use their faces to show emotions such as anger and playfulness.

The bold colors on a male mandrill's face tell other members of his troop just how strong and important he is. When he bares his enormous teeth he's saying, "Don't mess with me!"

QUICK, SCRAM!

Gunnison's prairie dogs are smarter than they look. With one call they warn their friends of an impending hawk attack—and the group looks up before scattering. A different call signals "coyote" and the gang make for the safety of their burrows.

UNWELCOME GUESTS

PARASITES

Welcome to the world of the meanest, most selfish of all creatures—the pathetic parasites. These lazy lowlife take their food directly from other, living animals—often hurting them.

Once settled upon, or inside, another animal (called the host), pesky parasites have got an easy life, absorbing food and making a comfortable home for themselves. The problem comes when it's time to reproduce. Getting eggs or babies from one host to another can be a challenge, especially if home is someone's gut, liver, or even brain. Despite those difficulties, there are parasites aplenty out there, mostly invisible to our eyes.

The body swells with blood.
A female louse can lay up to 300 eggs.
A human body louse feeds on human blood.

Bed fellows

Dust mites join you in your bed at night, but don't complain. These little creatures munch their way through all your dead skin cells. You could count about two million of them in one bed! Bed bugs, however, are not such helpful bedfellows: they feed on human blood!

Ripley's Believe It or Not!®

That's disgusting!

The larvae of the botfly burrow into live flesh and eat it. They often attack horses but can target humans. Aaron Dallas had five botfly larvae removed from his head, where he could hear and feel them moving around.

BIG WORD ALERT

INVERTEBRATE

Many parasites are invertebrates—that is animals without backbones, such as worms and fleas.

ONE AND ALL

The candiru is a parasitic fish of the Amazon. It swims up a person's penis and settles down in the bladder, where pee, or urine, is stored. The poor host will need surgery soon, or face death.

Sinus flukes (similar to leeches) burrow into the brains of whales.

One of the most dangerous parasites in the world is a rat flea that carries bubonic plague. This is a disease that was common long ago, and caused around 25 million human deaths in Europe alone.

Roundworms, or nematodes, are some of the most abundant animals on the planet. There are more than 20,000 species and many of them are parasites, living in the guts of other animals.

A cat flea can leap over 13 inches. That's like a human jumping to the top of a skyscraper in a single leap. Fleas can also keep jumping for days without taking a break.

Twist it!

TERRIBLE TICKS!

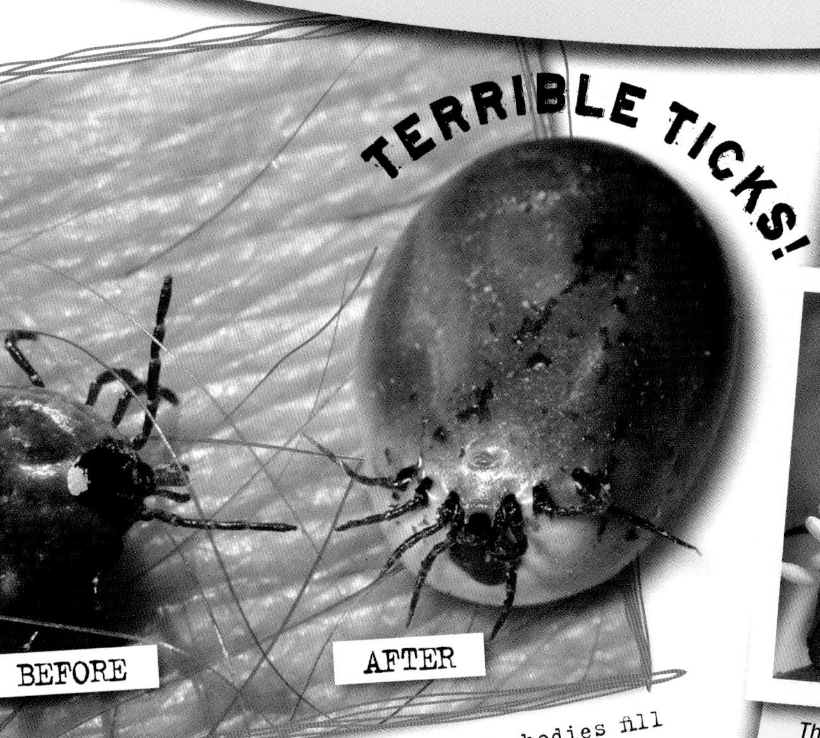

Ticks suck up so much blood that their bodies fill up like a balloon. They can't fly or jump, but they carry many diseases that are deadly to humans.

Vile!

This putrid sight is actually lice feeding on the skin of a giant grey whale.

Eaten from the inside out!

Parasitic wasps make sure their babies have plenty to eat, by laying their eggs inside, or on, a caterpillar's body! When the eggs hatch, the tiny larvae don't have to bother searching for fresh food.

The wasp lays its eggs all over the poor caterpillar.

Gross!

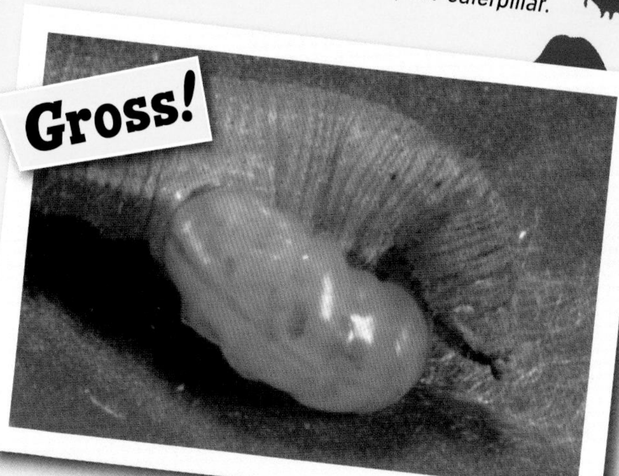

After eating the caterpillar's guts and juices, a wasp larva bursts out of its skin!

SWARM!

SAFETY IN NUMBERS

Desert locusts are loners, until they run out of food. Then, their brains produce a special friendship chemical called seratonin.

The locusts get an urge to hang out together—often in their billions! The giant gang then guzzles its way through millions of tons of food.

When a bunch of animals all get together they are called a swarm. Swarming happens because there is safety in numbers. When birds or fish gather in their thousands they buddy-up like one mighty monster. Each animal copies what its neighbor is doing, and the giant mass of moving flesh is more than a match for most predators.

KEY FACTS

- The time of year, the season, and weather conditions can all play a part in swarming behavior.
- Swarming is a good idea if lots of your favorite food is ripe and ready to eat for just a short time. You can gobble it all up!
- Some swarms have bosses. These leaders communicate with the rest of the gang, telling them where to go and what to do.

BIRDS OF A FEATHER FLOCK TOGETHER

Never was that more true than in the case of red-billed queleas. These seed-eating African birds number more than half a billion, and one flock can hold hundreds of millions of birds. When they settle on trees to strip off the fruit, the queleas' combined weight can break branches.

IT'S A STING THING

Giant swarms of stinging jellyfish, like these thimble jellyfish, are bad news for swimmers. They are becoming more common as oceans warm up.

Dr. Norman Gary is an insect scientist who tours the world with his Thriller Bee Show. While he plays the "bee flat" clarinet as many as 100,000 bees swarm all over him, even entering his mouth. Dr Gary is a bee expert who has written hundreds of scientific papers on his favorite subject, and has even trained bees to act in movies.

BEE FLAT

Locusts in a feeding frenzy can cause terrible food shortages and misery for humans as they strip crops bare.

twist it!

ONE AND ALL

Millions of salmon-pink flamingos gather at Lake Nakuru in Kenya to feed on the bacteria that live in the water. The birds get their pink color from their food.

King penguins can live together in enormous groups that number 600,000 or more.

In 1981, a swarm of 10 million krill, which are shrimp-like creatures that live in the ocean, collected near Antarctica. There were so many of them, the swarm could be seen from space! It was the largest swarm of any animal that has ever been known.

Periodical cicadas are bugs that survive for 17 years underground, then all emerge at the same time to breed. Males have a drum-like part of the body, which can be used to create a loud noise, to impress the females. When millions of cicadas swarm, the noise is so loud it's painful to the human ear.

Killer bees were created when scientists got different types of honeybees to mate. Twenty-six of the new, ferocious type of bee escaped from the laboratory and 40 years later had become established in the wild, creating enormous swarms. Although each sting is no worse than an ordinary bee sting, the killer insects are much more aggressive and likely to sting in large numbers, which can prove deadly.

BEAST BUDDIES

ANIMAL FRIENDS

BAILEY THE BUFFALO

Bailey the buffalo is not just a pet, he's treated like one of the family and is allowed to watch TV. He even eats at the kitchen table!

LION LOVER

Animal scientist Kevin Richardson loves lions, and is happy to cuddle up with them. He reckons it's easy to be friends with a lion, as long as you hang out with them while they are still cubs.

THE COBRA KING

King cobras are one of the world's most deadly snakes, but the Thai people of King Cobra Village keep them close to their hearts, literally! Most households keep a live cobra in a wooden box beneath their home, and get it out once a year for the village's three-day snake festival, when men fight the snakes and women dance with them.

HOTEL TRUNKS

Elephants are creatures of habit, and not particularly frightened of people. So they weren't bothered when a hotel was built across their route to some mango trees. Now hotel staff and guests stand back and watch while the elephants march through the hotel lobby to get to the ripe fruits!

THERE'S A HIPPO IN THE HOUSE!

How would you feel about adopting a wild animal? That's what a South African couple did when they found a newborn hippo, stranded and orphaned by floods. They named the cute little baby Jessica, and cared for her in their home while she grew, and grew, and GREW! Adult hippos weigh up to 3.5 tons, and can reach over 11 feet long, so Jessica had to leave home, and move in with a group of wild hippos that lived nearby!

WOLF MAN

Shaun Ellis is so comfortable in the company of wolves that he knows how to interact with them. He has studied their body language, facial expressions, and eating habits for years.

GOING, GOING, GONE

EVOLUTION AND EXTINCTION

One quarter of all mammals and one third of all amphibians (frogs, newts, and toads) are threatened with extinction, partly because humans are destroying animal habitats faster than ever before.

When people turn forests into farms or towns, and pollute natural environments, like the oceans and rivers, more and more animals die. Some species are killed for their skins and body parts, which are used in some traditional remedies. Other creatures are simply hunted for food or collected as pets.

LONESOME GEORGE

GIANT TORTOISE

BIG WORD ALERT

EXTINCT
When every last animal of a species has died, it has become extinct. Dinosaurs, dodos, and carrier pigeons are all extinct.

GHARIAL

10 of the most endangered species

Scientists believed Lonesome George was the last of his kind: a type of GIANT TORTOISE from the Galapagos Islands. However, after his death in 2012 scientists think there might be at least 17 other tortoises on the Islands that are similar to him.

In the last ten years, the number of GHARIALS has halved, plummeting to just 200 or so. These fish-eating crocodiles live in India and Nepal. They were once hunted for their skins, but are now critically endangered because their river habitats are being destroyed by humans.

All rhinos are in danger of extinction, but there are only about 50 JAVAN RHINOS left. Once there were thousands of these grass-grazers in Southeast Asia, but nearly all of them have been killed for their horns.

There are just 90 KAKAPOS left, and they are looked after by a group of scientists. Kakapos are the world's biggest parrots, and longest-living birds. They can't fly, which is why they nearly died out when people brought predators to their New Zealand home.

Gorillas are peaceful, plant-eating apes that live in African forests. All gorillas are endangered, but CROSS RIVER GORILLAS are especially rare because farms and roads are destroying their habitats. There are about 250 to 300 left.

The IBERIAN LYNX will probably be the first big cat to become extinct for at least 2,000 years. There are no more than 38 adult females left in the wild, and only around 110 wild Iberian lynxes altogether.

In 2004, a new species, the RAMESHWARAM PARACHUTE SPIDER, was discovered, but there are only a few hundred of these eight-legged creatures, and they live in a handful of plantations on an island near India.

SUMATRAN TIGERS are poisoned, hunted, trapped, and snared, and now there are less than 400 left in the wild. Also, the forests where they live are being turned into farms.

All over the world, the GIANT PANDA is used as a symbol for saving animals. There are about 1,600 pandas in the wild and they mostly eat bamboo. A panda baby is 1/900th the size of its mother, making it one of the smallest mammal babies.

A SOUTHERN BLUEFIN TUNA can live for 40 years and reach over 6 feet in length, if it doesn't get caught and eaten first. So many have been killed for food that they are now in serious danger of becoming extinct.

WILD ANIMALS INDEX

Bold numbers refer to main entries; numbers in *italic* refer to the illustrations

ACKNOWLEDGMENTS

COVER (l) Matt Rourke/AP/PA Photos, (r) © Gabriela Staebler/zefa/Corbis; **2** (c) © Olga Khoroshunova – fotolia.com, (b) Courtesy of Janice Wolf; **3** (t) © Eric Isselée – istockphoto.com, (r) Linda Cowen/Wolfpack Management; **4** © Gabriela Staebler/zefa/Corbis; **5** (t/r) Matt Rourke/AP/PA Photos; **6** © Tobias Bernhard/zefa/Corbis; **7** (t) NHPA/Photoshot, (c) Used by permission of Rodney Fox, (b/r) © Oceans Image/Photoshot, (b) © Jeffrey L. Rotman/Corbis; **8** (sp) Neil Bromhall/www.photolibrary.com; **9** (t/l, b/l) Peter Scoones/ Science Photo Library, (r) © Olga Khoroshunova – fotolia.com, (b/r) Gregory Ochocki/Science Photo Library; **10** © NHPA/Photoshot; **11** (c) © ktsdesign – fotolia.com, (t) Adrian Bicker/Science Photo Library, (r) © NHPA/Photoshot; **12** © Shusuke Sezai/epa/Corbis, (r) Oceans-Image/Photoshot; **13** (t/l) Karl H. Switak/Science Photo Library, (t/r) Tom McHugh/Science Photo Library, (b) © Larry Williams/Corbis; **14** (t) © N & B – fotolia.com, (b) © NHPA/Photoshot; **14–15** (l) Courtesy of Janice Wolf; **15** (c) Ministry of Fisheries via Getty Images, (b, r) © NHPA/Photoshot; **16–17** Jim Zipp/Science Photo Library; **17** (r) © NHPA/Photoshot, (t) Rexford Lord/ Science Photo Library, (b) Eric Gay/AP/PA Photos; **18** (b) © Eric Isselée – istockphoto.com, (sp) © Remi Benali/Corbis; **19** (l) © filip put – istockphoto.com, (r) Reuters/Ho New; **20** © DLILLC/Corbis; **20–21** (b) © N & B – fotolia.com; **21** (t) © Anthony Bannister/Gallo Images/Corbis, (b) Andy Rouse/Rex Features; **22** (b/l) © John Anderson – fotolia.com, (sp) David B Fleetham/www.photolibrary.com, (t, t/r) © NHPA/Photoshot; **23** (t/c/l, t/c/r, t/r) © NHPA/Photoshot, (b) © Roger Garwood & Trish Ainslie/Corbis; **24** Eye Of Science/ Science Photo Library; **25** (bgd) George Bernard/Science Photo Library (t/l) Mark Fairhurst/UPPA/Photoshot, (b/l) Cheryl Power/Science Photo Library, (t/c) Eye Of Science/Science Photo Library, (t/r) Alan Sirulnikoff/Science Photo Library, (b/r) Pasieka/Science Photo Library; **26** Manoj Shah/Getty Images; **27** (t/l) © Paul Stock – fotolia.com, (t/c, t/r) Satoshi Kuribayashi/www.photolibrary.com, (c) Bournemouth News/Rex Features, (b/r) Maurice Tibbles/www.photolibrary.com; **28** (l) © NHPA/Photoshot, (r) © sunset man – fotolia.com; **29** (l, r, t, t/c) © NHPA/Photoshot; **30** (t) © Eky Chan – fotolia.com, (r) Frank Lukasseck/Getty Images; **31** (t, b) © NHPA/ Photoshot; **32** (l) James Balog/Imagebank/Getty Images, (b) © Yaroslav Gnatuk – fotolia.com, (t) David Doubilet/National Geographic/ Getty Images; **33** (t) © Holger Mette – fotolia.com, (b) © NHPA/Photoshot; **34** (b) Mark Newman/FLPA, (t) Hiroya Minakuchi/Minden Pictures/FLPA; **35** (l) © NHPA/Photoshot, (b/r) Michael K. Nichols/National Geographic/Getty Images, (t) John Beatty/Science Photo Library; **36** (l) © Kitch Bain – fotolia.com, (c) © Karen Roach – fotolia.com, (b/l) © The physicist – fotolia.com; **37** (t/l) Michael Nichols/National Geographic/Getty Images, (c) Gail Shumway/Taxi/Getty Images, (r) © RebeccaAnne – fotolia.com; **38** (l) © NHPA/ Photoshot, (r) Darlyne A. Murawski/National Geographic/Getty Images; **39** (l) © Dwight Davis – fotolia.com, (b/l) Ken Lucas/Getty Images, (c) © Heinz Waldukat – fotolia.com, (t) © Henrik Larsson – fotolia.com, (c/r) © Stephen Bonk – fotolia.com, (b/r) Robert F. Sisson/National Geographic/Getty Images; **40** (l) Oceans-Image/Photoshot, (r) Bildagentur RM/www.photolibrary.com; **40–41** (bgd) David Shale/www.photolibrary.com; **41** (t/r) Sipa Press/Rex Features; **42** (l) Carlo Allegri/Getty Images, (b) Photograph by Falise Thierry/Gamma/Eyedea/Camera Press London, (c) Zoom/Barcroft Media; **43** (t/l, r) Zoom/Barcroft Media, (b) Linda Cowen/Wolfpack Management; **44** (l) © siloto – fotolia.com, (c) Reuters/Guillermo Granja; **45** (t/l) Tony Camacho/Science Photo Library, (l) Sue Flood/ Getty Images, (b/r) © Timothy Lubcke – fotolia.com, (c/r) © ImagineImages – fotolia.com, (t/r) © dzain – fotolia.com

Key: t = top, b = bottom, c = center, l = left, r = right, sp = single page, dp = double page, bgd = background

Every attempt has been made to acknowledge correctly and contact copyright holders and we apologize in advance for any unintentional errors or omissions, which will be corrected in future editions.